CRAIG HALLORAN

THE SUPERNATURAL
BOUNTY
HUNTER
FILES

HOLY SMOKE
BOOK 8

Holy Smoke
The Supernatural Bounty Hunter Series: Book 8
By Craig Halloran

TWO-TEN BOOK PRESS
P.O. Box 4215, Charleston, WV 25364

ISBN eBook: 978-1-941208-48-9
ISBN Paperback: 978-1-941208-49-6

http://www.thedarkslayer.net

Edited by Cherise Kelley

Publisher's Note
This book is a work of fiction. Names, characters, places, and incidents either are the product of the author's imagination or are used fictitiously, and any resemblance to actual persons, living or dead, events, or locales is entirely coincidental.

CHAPTER 1

FORT CARROLL SAT IN THE middle of the Patapsco River like a ghost city. Smoke and Sid were at the docks where the FBI had dropped off Titus Tolliver days earlier. Beside the phantom black Dodge Hellcat, Sid squeezed into the sweetheart suit. Her skin tingled. A coppery taste filled her mouth. She fought the urge to spit.

"You okay?" Smoke's sweetheart suit only covered him above the waist. The refined sinew coating his muscular frame rippled with every movement. He blew into a small inflatable raft they were going to stow their weapons and gear in. "You look a little nervous." He gazed at the river. "It's not the easiest swim."

Sid loosened up her arms by doing small windmills. She cracked her neck from side to side. "I was feeling a little tight, but I'm feeling better with the suit on. I bet I can beat you over there."

"Hey, I'm hauling all the gear." Smiling, he shoved a pair of guns into the floating sack. He stood up with a knife and belt in his hand, wrapped it around Sid's waist, and fastened it with a snap. Backing up, he said with an approving nod, "You've got that Bond girl thing going on. I like it."

"Bond girls aren't half the woman I am. They're scrawny."

Smoke put his arms around her waist. "And not half as sexy."

"Why don't I take a picture?" Sam, Smoke's sister, was dressed in black, grey, and white camouflage. Her hair was pulled back in a long ponytail. Guppy stood beside her, dressed the same, with a grin on his face. His black truck was parked behind them. Sam pulled out her phone. "You two look so adorable together. No one would ever suspect you're a couple of lunatics."

"I'd rather you didn't. This isn't the best place for a flash," Sid said.

"OK, fine." Sam put her phone away. Looking around, she said, "So what about this Vormus guy? Isn't he supposed to be here?"

"He said he'd meet us on the island," Smoke said.

"And doesn't that seem a little suspicious, coming from a guy who tried to kill us all?" Sam replied.

Smoke shrugged.

"Are you okay with this, Sid?" Sam asked.

Adjusting her knife belt, she said, "I have to find out where my niece and sister are."

"I don't like it," Sam said, "but if you don't make it back, I promise to take care of the Hellcat. The keys are in it, right?"

Sid laughed. "You're more than welcome, Sis."

"Aw, come here." Sam clomped over on her high

heels and gave Sid a firm hug. "You'd better make it back. That place is creepy out there. I can just imagine all those monsters spilling outside."

"And I can't imagine you running from them in those high heels."

"Oh, I won't be running. I'll be driving the Hellcat." Sam made a cat sound.

"Boy, you really do want my car, don't you!" Sid said.

"I'm sorry, I have to say funny things when I'm nervous." Sam shouted at Guppy, "You make sure they've got everything Mal gave you?"

"I did," Guppy replied.

"Well, double check it."

"I did."

"Triple—"

"Done!"

"You're a good friend and sister, Sam. We'll make it back."

Sam swatted at a mosquito buzzing near her face. "I hate mosquitos." Stepping away from Sid, she said, "Guppy, I've got a mosquito."

Sam's burly husband sauntered over with an aerosol can. He sprayed mist around Sam. "Don't get it in my mouth," she said, adding a little cough.

Smoke slung the inflatable pack over his shoulder. "I guess it's time." He and Sid walked toward the boat ramp at Hawkins Point. There wasn't anyone else around. He said to Sam, "We'll be back before dawn."

"You'd better be."

Sid and Smoke waded into the cold waters of the river, sending shivers up from her bare feet.

Smoke handed her a pair of flippers. "These will make the swim a lot easier."

"You know, I didn't even think of that. I guess I should have expected this from a former frogman."

He snapped his green-lensed goggles over his head. "What can I say. I love the water. So are you ready?"

As the waters splashed against the rocks from the wake of a barge passing by, she waded in deeper. With a nod, she eyed Fort Carroll. Her heart pounded. Even though the sweetheart suit sent steady energy into her body, there was quavering inside. It was a long swim. Even longer thinking about the unknown that waited for them on the island. She slipped on her goggles. "See if you can keep up."

"Hah!" Smoke submerged himself to the neck. With the floating sack tethered to his waist, he swam alongside her. His strokes were long and steady. He cut through the water like a great fish.

Sidney pushed off on a rock. The sweetheart suit gave a little extra buoyancy, and the flippers helped a lot. It didn't take long for her freestyle stroke to get into rhythm.

Boy, I wish I could have swum with these on swim team.

Smoke edged out in front, glancing back from time to time. Before long, they were halfway to the fort. With her competitive instinct kicking in, she swam faster. Her long fingers chopped and pushed through the water, but no matter how hard she tried, she couldn't catch Smoke.

Good Lord, he's fast.

A spotlight hit the waters nearby. It came from Fort Carroll.

CHAPTER 2

S MOKE STOPPED. THEY BOTH TREADED water. The spotlight brushed over the waves. Its beam came from just over the fort's fortification wall. The bright lens moved from side to side, just west of them.

"Get behind me," Smoke said. "When I say duck, go under."

"Okay."

The beam cruised right toward them.

"Duck."

After taking a small breath, Sid half swam, half sank into the water. Smoke did the same. The two hovered just below the black water's surface. The light cruised over their location. The illumination wavered above. The light searching for them was the only hopeful sight in the blackness.

The beam moved on.

Smoke took her hand and led them up. Resurfacing, she gasped for air. Smoke's head panned left and right. Her head was on a swivel. The searchlight was gone.

"What do you think?" she whispered.

"I don't see anything." Smoke's stare was fixed on the wall where the light had come from. "Nothing at all. Even with the goggles."

Treading water and taking a breath, she said, "We need to keep moving. This water's choppier than I figured."

Smoke's eyes lit up. "Are you getting tired?"

She nodded.

He pushed the sack over to Sid. "Use this. Besides, we need to take our time if eyes are watching."

"Fair enough." She took a breath. "I didn't think I'd get so winded. At least not with the suit on."

"We're fighting a current. Most of the time, when you fight the water, it wins. Let's go."

They swam at half the speed they had been. Before long, Sid got a second wind. She pushed it again, legs kicking faster just under the water. Ten more minutes' hard swimming and they both hit the stony base of the old fort's rim. She climbed up on the ledge and sat. Chest heaving, she caught her breath.

"It's not the asthma, is it?" Smoke asked.

"Maybe a little." She rolled her shoulder. "Man, that was a swim."

"Going back will be easier." Smoke remained in the water, staring up at the fort's stone walls. The large cut stones, stacked eight high, made a wall much higher than expected. "We'll need to ease around the rim and find a spot to squeeze into."

Sid remembered the long gaps between the stones. She stared at Hawkins Point, where they had started out.

It looked far away. She eased back into the water. "After you, John."

Hugging the fort's base, they moved hand over hand, eyeing the top of the wall. Sid read a marker: PRIVATE. KEEP OFF. GUARD DOG.

Eyeing the same thing, Smoke said, "And I thought we only had to worry about shifters."

"You worry about shifters? I don't."

He kept working his way around the wall. "And that's why you wear the pants in this family."

They came to a stop at a lower section of the outer wall, where there was a big break between the stones. Smoke helped Sid up into it. He climbed up after her. With the water splashing against the walls, he looked around. "Creepy."

"Just like the magazine. Sometimes I feel like I'm on the cover." She slipped through the gap, climbing up the broken wall, and made it to ground level. The eerie island was covered in dry trees and brown bushes run amok. None looked like anything she'd seen before. "Strange place for things to grow."

"Life finds a way everywhere." Smoke found a spot where the bushy ground gave way to a clearing on the old pavement. Still huddled behind the brush, he opened the waterproof sack. He and Sid strapped on their guns. They'd loaded the magazines earlier. Red tips at the top. Blue and green tips in the bottom. Smoke was smiling.

"Getting a little excited, are you?"

"Sometimes I feel a little giddy among the uncanny." He holstered both his weapons. From inside the sack, he pulled out a small bottle. He rattled the pills inside.

Sid couldn't hide her surprise. "More supervitamins in stock?"

"I think Mal likes to pretend he's low. He thinks we'll hoard them all."

"Did he say that?"

"No, but I can tell." Something buzzed inside the sack. Smoke produced a phone. "It's for you."

It was a message from Sam: "Status?" followed by several concerned emojis.

Sid texted her back. "Doing great." She tossed the phone in the sack. "Better leave it."

Smoke swallowed a vitamin.

"Isn't this a little premature?"

Rolling his finger in front of his face he said, "It's got a special coating, and I can do my regurgitation thing. I'd love to teach you."

Sid's face crinkled. "I know you're my husband and I need to accept you as you are, but that doesn't mean I have to like everything you do." She opened her hand. "The old-fashioned way will be just fine."

He gave her two pills. "It doesn't bother you too much, does it?"

"I'll say this: better hope nothing I ever feed you comes up again at the dinner table."

"Ha ha. I'm pretty sure that won't happen. You're an excellent cook." He sniffed. "Do I smell lasagna?"

She rolled her eyes. "Let's go."

Even though they were wearing the sweetheart suits and armed to the teeth, her belly had still quavered until a minute ago. Smoke had a way of easing the tension. The rugged man was fearless in the eye of anything he faced. She had no doubt there was something special about him.

They picked their way through the fort, staying hidden in the trees and brush. The center of the compound was cleared off. Someone had used the spotlight, but there weren't any other signs or sounds of people. A chilling thought came to mind. Perhaps there was a shifter on guard, skulking in the brush, waiting to pounce.

And then Sid went to step over a heap on the ground and froze. It was a body. Sid squatted down and gasped. The man's head was twisted past his shoulder, and his dead hands gripped a spotlight.

CHAPTER 3

SID COULDN'T FIGHT THE SHIVERS that made her hairs stand on end. The man's head brought back thoughts of Adam Vaughn, the wolf man. He'd killed her supervisor, Jack Dydeck, and many other agents in the same horrific fashion. This time, there wasn't all that blood.

She looked back for Smoke. He was gone. She whipped out her weapon. The Glock quelled her earlier fears. Her dark eyes searched the night. A scuffle in the brush caught her ear. She turned and took aim.

Two men approached.

"Don't take another step," she commanded.

"Which is it?" said the man in front with his hands up. "He says march and you say halt." It was Vormus. The vampire shifter's white hair was tied back in a ponytail. He wore large sunglasses and grey slacks, and his lavender sweater stood out against his alabaster skin. "Well?"

Keeping her gun on him, Sid said, "Did you kill this guy?"

"No, one of those raccoons did," Vormus said in his formal and condescending manner.

Smoke shoved his gun into Vormus's back. "Answer the lady."

"Of course I did."

"If you're going to work with us, you need to stop killing people." Sid stood up. "We aren't murderers."

"Pfft. If you're going to take that attitude, then you've lost. These guards, they know what side of the fence they are on. They have it coming as much as anyone else. Nobility." Vormus lifted a brow. "I was raised with nobility. Neither of you have any idea what that is. No one in this heap of a country does. Here, everyone thinks they're so special."

Vormus made a good point. It was something Sid had contemplated more than once. Some of the people they fought were just doing a job. It made it tough when she had to deal with them. Sometimes if you left a man alive, you might lose your own. How do you fight a secret war that is off the books? But they had to know what was going on. They had made a choice.

"Compared to you, most all of us are special." Sid holstered her gun. "How'd you get here?"

"I jumped off the Francis Scott Key Bridge. You should have seen the faces those brats made when I jumped. Oh, how I wish I could still find the joy in that." He dusted off his hands. "So I floated down here. About an hour later I noticed your little party across the way. That dead man had a watchful eye, too, so I ended him."

She tilted her head. "Too? You mean there are more dead?"

Looking at his nails, Vormus said, "Maybe a couple. What? You should be thanking me. It's not on your conscience, it's on mine." He leaned back and said to Smoke, "But we both know I don't have one."

"You have something," Smoke said, "Or you wouldn't be helping us."

Taking a glance at the dead man's body, the shifter replied, "He means as much to me as, what do you special ones call it, ah, as killroad means to you."

"It's roadkill," she said. "Smoke, do you want to scout around before we take this investigation any deeper?"

"I've cleared the area," Vormus said.

"Sit down," Smoke replied.

"Here? On the ground?"

Smoke drove his boot into the back of Vormus's knee.

The shifter collapsed, but he popped right up again. Fangs bared, he got in Smoke's face. "Don't take my cooperation as softness. I might not feel much, but I still have a temper. Take warning, John Smoke. Don't treat me like chattel."

Staring Vormus in the eye, Smoke said, "You're worse than chattel. Don't forget it."

Vormus sneered.

"I've got this, John," Sid said.

Smoke gave a quick nod and moved out of sight.

Facing Sid, Vormus said, "It's only a matter of time before he embraces what he is. The deeper you go down this Lewis Carroll rabbit hole, the more his true nature will reveal itself. It's the same for the both of you."

"It's not something we can avoid?"

"No, you can't. Sidney, I'm grateful you have shown me a degree of trust. After all, we both want the same thing. You need to save your sister. I need to save myself. I'm sincere about that."

"I'll be convinced when my sister and niece are out of harm's way." Keeping her eyes on Vormus, she said, "How do I know she's not a shifter already?"

"I know there is much to discuss on that, and I don't have any intent to be vague, but there is a proving ground. It takes time to show commitment."

"What sort of proving ground?"

"Think of what you know about a gang's initiation. Multiply by ten."

"Are you saying she'll have to kill somebody?"

"I'm saying she will kill somebody, and somebody could be anybody. It could be somebody close to her. It was for me."

"Who did you kill?"

"My parents."

"You don't mean that."

"You have every reason to believe I'm a liar, but I'm not, as I have no reason to lie. But you have to kill someone dear to you. I've known shifters who even took out their own children." His stone-cold stare didn't change. "They didn't shed a tear."

Megan.

Two thoughts coursed through Sid's mind. First, Allison wasn't the best mother to begin with. She was selfish by nature, and she never gave Megan the attention she should. Second, Vormus, if all he said was true, deserved to die. He didn't deserve redemption of any kind. But she needed him. She didn't like it.

Smoke glided back into view. "It's clear. Everything good here?"

"Peachy," she replied. She turned to Vormus. "Where to?"

"You're asking me? This is the first time I've been here too. I'm not much of what you call an investigator. I just know who to fetch when we get in there, wherever there is."

"I've got it," Smoke said. "There's a boat docked on the bridge side. It's got to be close to where they go in. Follow me."

"After you," she said, waving her gun at Vormus.

CHAPTER 4

T HE THREE-AND-A-HALF-ACRE ISLAND FORT DIDN'T prove difficult to navigate. Amid a small crane covered in vines and a Bobcat loader with a busted tread, Smoke found a path beaten down by human traffic. It led down a staircase into a network of tunnels and stone archways. The ground was muddy and wet, filled with silt from the bay. Critters scattered in the darkness.

Sid's goggles enhanced her sight enough to make out the faint outlines of the walls. The forms of Vormus and Smoke were clear. Still, it was a little unsettling moving in the pitch-black without a single source of light.

Smoke engaged the laser sight on his pistol.

Good idea.

Sid did the same.

The red beams cut through the darkness, tracing the walls, giving them the appearance of something real and not some maze hidden in the night.

Smoke moved with his eyes low, burrowing farther into the tunnel. He stepped up on a ledge that led into another alcove. The storage chamber of the old fort was big enough to hold about twenty men. There was nothing inside except the stainless steel frame of an elevator.

"You've got to be kidding me," Sid said, stepping forward and inspecting the frame. "An elevator? Here? Huh, it needs a proxy card."

Smoke dangled a proxy card in front of her eyes. "I patted down one of Vormus's dead guards." He went to scan it. "Going down, I suppose?"

She stopped him. "If this place is so important, shouldn't it be under heavier guard?"

"Again, the shifters are overconfident," Vormus said.

"Huh," said Sid, "and who's to say there isn't some other way out? They probably have a tunnel under here that leads to the Pentagon."

"You mean the Pentagragon," Smoke added.

"Don't start." She brushed a strand of wet hair from her eye. "Of course, at this point, nothing would surprise me." She filled both hands with pistol grips and took a breath.

Smoke scanned the card.

The doors parted. A small halogen bulb inside the elevator was a beacon of bright light. Head turned aside, Sid stepped in. Vormus and Smoke joined her. The new illumination gave her a close look at Vormus's slacks and sweater. "What's with you and lavender?"

"It was a dear aunt's favorite color."

"Did you kill her, too?"

"No, something else did."

"OTIS," Smoke said, eyeing the lettering at the top of the elevator panel. "Wow, they make elevators everywhere. I bet contractors know a lot more than they should." He glanced down. There were two buttons, one over the other. "Going down?" Smoke said with a Steven Tyler chuckle.

"Funny, just don't bust out the air guitar," Sid said. The doors closed. The elevator began to move. Her adrenaline surged.

With a quizzical expression, Vormus asked, "What's an air guitar?"

Sid's fingers rubbed her clammy palms. The elevator ride was either really long or really slow. She looked up but away from the light. She'd toured an elevator shaft when she was a girl. She'd been amazed at how deep it went and how dark it was. Her skin had crawled the entire time. There was only one way out. What if that way failed?

"It's deep," Smoke said. "It has to be deeper than the bay. At least fifty feet."

"How could anyone make such a thing without anyone noticing?" she replied. "This is worse than Mallows Bay."

Vormus snorted. "You haven't seen everything man can do. You only see what is in the world above. They let you see that. Evil lurks in the depths where the light is not wanted. You'd be astonished what is buried in Europe and beneath the great pyramids." He made an effort to chuckle. "And not just mummies."

The elevator stopped with a wobble. Sid lifted both barrels toward the exit. The stainless steel doors parted. Her lips did too. "Morning glory."

CHAPTER 5

I<small>T WAS A CAVERNOUS VIEW</small>. Sid couldn't see from one side to the other. Steel girders held up a dome roof made of yellow concrete block. The cavern floor was solid rock and uneven in many places. The stone was slick with a thin sheen of water. Metal lanterns with glass bulbs and dim yellow gas lights grafted to the walls and hanging above gave off an eerie glow. The air she breathed was damp. It made Sidney think of a subway tunnel but a dozen times bigger.

Smoke stepped out. His broad back blocked her view. She nudged him forward. His head turned in all directions. Under his breath, he said, "It's like the Batcave."

"More like a watery tomb."

Vormus stepped into the cavern. The elevator doors closed. "Interesting, I don't see anyone."

Careful where she stepped, Sid moved forward with Smoke, toward the center of the room. There were desks similar to something one would see in a World War II army base. The rest of the wooden furniture appeared to be two hundred years old. Damp papers lay on the desks and floors. There were old glass-panel cubicles against the walls on the right. She noticed something familiar and gave Smoke a nudge.

The coffin they had put Titus Tolliver in lay on the floor. Smoke kneeled down and picked up a pair of flex cuffs that had been snipped. "At least we know he made it in here."

"True, but where, exactly? It doesn't look like anyone has been in here in days."

The sound of metal being struck echoed in the great chamber. It came again. In the vast open space, the sound's source was hard to make out.

Head tilted and eyes closed, Sid said, "It sounds like someone tossing a rock through a ventilation duct."

"Just bigger," Smoke added.

"Maybe the rats are much bigger down here," Vormus suggested.

"There wouldn't be any rats down here. Well, not unless you've met Swift Venison. Could he be down here?" she asked.

"They might all be," Smoke said.

The tapping became steady.

"That's Morse code," Smoke said. He cupped is ear.

Vormus opened his mouth to speak. Sid shushed him.

"Left," Smoke said, heading that direction with Sid and Vormus in tow. He came to a stop at the edge of a metal trapdoor. It was about four feet by four in size. The hinges were heavy iron. Flush to the floor, the door was a solid plate, aside from a large keyhole.

Sid noted more metal tombs. There were dozens, spaced out evenly and lined up all the way to the yellow block walls. "Geez, I hope these things aren't full of shifters."

"That would be a lot of shifters." Smoke kneeled down and looked in the keyhole. "I think I see an eyeball." He leaned closer. "Yup, it's an eyeball." He rapped his knuckles on the door. The same knock came back.

"Any ideas?" she said to Vormus.

The vampire shifter shrugged. "I suppose you'll just have to open up the box."

"I'll see what I can find." Sid made her way to the desks and sorted through the papers, which were old and damaged. There was Drake letterhead on what appeared to be invoices and shipping manifests. The contents weren't described. It was just a list of packages. She opened desk drawers and rummaged through them. She found several fountain pens. "Huh, I bet these are worth some money."

Vormus puckered a brow. "A pen?"

"An antique pen."

"Yes, but still, just a pen. I can't imagine it would have any notable value."

"Why don't you quit standing around in your Barney sweater and help me look for a key?"

"Who's Barney?"

"Just look."

Vormus began milling about in imitation of what Sid was doing. He didn't seem to have any idea what doing real work was like. She made her way over to the glass-paned cubicles on the right side of the cavern, where she found a clipboard hanging by a nail hammered into the wooden frame of a cubicle. There was a gridded box with names on it. "Oh, snap."

"What?" Vormus said in her ear. He'd crept right up on her heels.

She shoved him back with an elbow. "Don't ever do that again."

He inhaled through his nose. "Your hair smells nice. What kind of shampoo do you use? It has a floral luster to it that I like."

Sid's eyes were fixed on the page. Her lips said the words but not out loud.

Angi Harlow.

Swift Venison.

Adam Vaughn.

There were others. Among them in fresh ink was Titus Tolliver. She headed back toward Smoke and lined up the grid boxes from the clipboard sheet with the ones on the floor. They matched up.

Smoke glanced up at her. "What's up?"

"I think I have a prison manifest."

"Really?" He made his way over and checked it out. "I had a feeling they weren't dead. Well, maybe we can finish them up now."

"I told you shifters weren't easy to kill," Vormus stated. "It's our thing."

"Everything dies eventually." Smoke fingered the manifest. "So who do we have communicating in this box here? Ah, our old buddy Toad Man. Remember him?"

"How could I forget?"

"He's the one pecking inside. Did you find a key?"

"No." Sid paced along the trapdoors. She lingered over the one with Adam Vaughn's name. He'd killed her friends. He should be dead. She pointed her gun down at the keyhole and noticed it was turned to three o'clock. "Smoke."

He slid over and gave a nod. He grabbed the handle on the door. Sid stood on the other side with her gun ready. She gave him a nod. He lifted the trapdoor. Nothing popped out, jumped, or scurried from the hole. The chamber wasn't very deep, but it was empty. Just a metal door over a stone hole.

They checked all the locks in this row. All of them were unlocked except for the one marked "Toad Man Eugene Green."

She tossed Vormus the manifest. "Who was the one you were looking for?"

"Ah, the keeper of secrets, Manson Bay." He pecked his neatly trimmed fingernail on the clipboard. "It says he's here. A good thing." Vormus pointed. "Three over."

She moved. "It's unlocked." The eerie quietness in the room bothered her. They weren't quiet, and their presence had to be easily known. No one else, if they were there, was scratching or pecking.

Smoke came over and took her hand. With a nod from Sid, he opened the small prison.

"Empty," she said.

"That's disappointing," Vormus replied.

One by one, they opened all the doors. Every cell was unlocked and empty aside from the one with Toad Man. The three of them surrounded it.

"I don't know if this is a good thing or bad." She sighed. "If we want answers, we're going to need a key. Let's keep looking."

Toad Man

CHAPTER 6

WHILE SIDNEY AND VORMUS SEARCHED for a key, Smoke sat on the trapdoor, knocking his knuckle on the metal in Morse code. The person inside the tomb pecked back. "So far as I can tell, it's Toad Man. He's angry."

Talking loudly from across the cavern, Sid said, "Why isn't he talking?"

"I think this metal is too thick. Sounds are probably muffled. I don't know. Any luck with a key?"

"No." Sid searched everything there was to search. She looked under desks. Pulled out drawers. Turned over tables. She looked through shelves of rations and supplies. There wasn't a key of any kind. Worry set in. The captured shifters had been here, and now they were gone without a trace. She wondered why they might have been moved. Or were they still inside the cavern, just elsewhere? "Vormus, did you find anything?"

Somewhere inside the underground complex, Vormus said, "As regards a key, no."

Sid stepped outside the wood-and-glass cubicle. She didn't see Vormus. "Where are you?"

"South of you. In the shadows where the walls of block turn to solid stone. There are some smaller offshoot caves down here. Possibly a tunnel, but it looks quite small."

"I got it," Smoke said.

Sid hustled over to him and asked, "You got what?"

Smoke lay flat on his belly. His hands were filled with slender metal tools. He worked the keyhole. Metal scratched on metal. The keyhole clicked. "We're open for business now."

"Toad Man, huh? I wonder if he'll be excited to see us," she said with a smile.

"I have to admit, I'm looking forward to seeing his face." Smoke took the handle.

Sid readied her gun.

Smoke opened the door.

Slowly, Eugene Green, Toad Man, crawled out. All he wore was a pair of jeans, but his skin was brush brown and clumpy. Even in man form, his eyes were extremely large. They widened when Smoke removed the gag from his mouth and he said, "You!"

"How are you doing, Eugene?" Sid said.

Eugene's frog neck turned toward her. "You too?" He gathered himself into a dangerous crouching position. His thick legs coiled to spring. "I can't believe it's you. Of all the despicable people. I swore if I ever saw you again, I'd bury you both."

Smoke lowered his gun to aim between Toad Man's

eyes. "That's not a nice thing to say to someone who just let you out of captivity, now is it?"

Blinking, Eugene said, "I don't care. I still hate you both." His long tongue flicked from his mouth. He had a little tic when he talked. Slowly he pointed at the both of them. "I hate you and you. You got me put in this hole. They called me a failure. Took my glory. My money. My everything."

"We don't care," Sid said. "What happened to the others? Why did they leave you here?"

"What do you mean?" Eugene looked around. His jaw dropped. "Oh my. Are all the others gone?" He scanned his surroundings. "Where did everyone go? Did you kill them all?"

Smoke popped the ugly frogman on the top of the head with the butt of his pistol. "Don't play stupid, toad neck."

Wincing, Eugene rubbed his neck with his long toad fingers. "Beat me all you want." His tongue snapped in and out. "I can take it. I'll heal. I'll be damned if I help you with anything."

"Then you're going back in the hole." Smoke gave him a shove.

"No, wait. At least let me breathe the air. Is that lilac I smell?" Eugene's small nostrils sniffed. "Lilac and bay water. It's funny, but women always have a smell." His eyes combed over Sid's body. He batted his lashes. "You're a fetching morsel. I could get over my hate if you were to—"

Smoke cracked him in the head again.

"Just put him in the hole. If he's not talking, we're wasting our time." Sid motioned to Smoke with her gun.

"Perhaps if he will not talk, I should deal with him." Vormus appeared.

Eugene moved away from Vormus. "What are you doing here?"

"That's my business, Toad Man." Vormus loomed over the smaller man. His eyes became hypnotic. "Tell me everything you know. Particularly about Manson Bay."

"Why are you asking me? You're further in than me." Eugene got all fidgety and sweaty. "I'm nothing. You're royalty."

Vormus pressed. "Where did they all go?"

"They locked me up. I don't know. You saw how they left me to rot." Needling his fingers, he shifted his bulging eyes between Smoke and Sid. "I don't play well with the others. They don't care for me. I never cared for their snobbery."

"You're testing my patience, amphibian," Vormus warned.

Toad Man pleaded. "Just take me to the top. To the top. Heh. I'll tell you all you need to know." His tongue licked out over his eye. "Or at least all I know. I swear it."

"Near a large body of water so you can squirt free? I don't think so." Vormus pushed up his sleeves, revealing his wiry forearms. He clamped his fingers around Eugene's neck. His eyes flashed, and he opened his mouth and expanded his jaws, revealing very long, sharp teeth.

Sid's hairs stood on end. Vormus had gone from

gentle snob to monster. She pointed the gun at his head, saying, "Vormus, what's going on?"

"I don't know." Vormus's eyes swirled. His features stretched.

The room started to spin. Sid's knees bent to keep her from falling. "Vormus?"

"Okay! Okay!" Eugene cried out. "I'll tell you everything. Just stay out of my mind. I hate that." He panted for breath. His body curled into fetal position. "I'd rather be in the hole than go through mind crap."

Vormus's contorted face resumed its natural state.

Sid swallowed. Her chest pounded. She'd seen Kane do something similar before when she was his captive. The man had an unexplainable power that went well beyond his dominating appearance. Apparently there was also more to Vormus than met the eye.

Smoke took her hand. His eyes were filled with concern.

She squeezed his hand.

"Out with it, Toad Man. Where are the others?" Vormus said.

"They set them free," Eugene said with a sob. "They set them all free but me."

CHAPTER 7

THE WORDS TOAD MAN SPOKE ignited Sid's inner
fire. "You mean to tell me they're all out there on
the loose again?"

The balled-up Toad Man nodded.

"Well, that just pisses me off," Sid said. Her words
were venom. "I'm going to kill Cyrus. We've been hauling
them in just so they can let them out again? What is this,
Guantanamo Bay? I could kill somebody!"

While Sid stormed through the chamber, Vormus
asked Eugene, "What about the Keeper of Secrets. He
was here, was he not?"

"He was. We all were," Toad Man said weakly. "They'd
let us out one by one to feed us. Beat us. Torment us."

"Who did that?" Smoke asked.

Eugene glared at Smoke. "The other shifters. You
know," he air quoted his fingers, "'the cherished ones.'
Please, please, please, just take me with you out there. I
don't want to slowly die down here."

"I didn't think shifters could die so easily."

Eugene scowled at Smoke. "Well, you haven't been

living in a hole!" His face softened. "Sorry, you must sympathize with my frustration. I've been stuck in a hole since you hauled me in. I'm bitter. Can you blame me?"

The lights flickered. Everyone froze. Their eyes looked up and down. The flames quavered once more.

Eyes up, Sid said, "I don't like this. We might not get out of here."

"Does this normally happen?" Smoke asked Eugene.

He shrugged. "I don't know. I'm in the hole all the time. Besides, you're deep. The light is not meant for the deep dark belly. Mortals aren't either."

"Toad Man, what is Kane up to?"

"He has plans. Big plans. That's why he let them all out. He needs them. All of them. He wants to restore his disrupted operations. You know, the ones these two ruined." Toad Man had a clear second set of lenses over his eyes when he blinked. "He says with them out of the picture, it will be business as usual."

"Well, we aren't out of the picture," Sid commented. She sat down on one of the old wooden office chairs. The thought of all the shifters they'd captured run amok out there made her sick.

"No, clearly you aren't out of the picture...yet."

"What's that supposed to mean?" she said.

"Just wishful thinking. So are you going to take me out there with you? Please. I'll try to control my tongue." He flicked the long thing in and out of his mouth. "It just isn't easy."

"You haven't told us anything useful," Smoke said. "No names. No locations. No nothing. Just big plans.

How gullible do you think we are? You're delaying. I'm just wondering what for."

Touching his chest, Eugene said, "Me? Delay? I'd never trifle with the likes of Vormus."

Something scurried in the blackness on the edges of the enormous cavern.

Sid got up off her chair so quickly she knocked it over. "Vormus, did you see anything over there?"

"A large burrow-like tunnel. I didn't have time to search it due to all the commotion."

Something slunk in the darkness. The lights flickered. The effect was more like a strobe light. Sid pointed her laser at the black spot. The beam died in the dark light.

"They move," Eugene said in a sinister whisper.

Backing toward Smoke, Sid said, "What moves?"

"The guardians. They wake from their slumber. They feast on the sweet marrow of mortals." Eugene hopped into the nearest cell in a single leap and slammed the door shut. "Goodbye, mortals!"

Smoke nudged up alongside Sid. "Stay close."

A centipede-like creature, thicker than a man's leg and longer than two, snaked out from the darkness. The plum-colored monster moved on thousands of silent legs. Its face had huge green eyes filled with many smaller lenses. A sharp horn was on its head. Double sets of black pinchers guarded the monster's mouth.

Smoke and Sid backed up. Sid said, "Vormus, have you seen one of these things before?"

"They call them the vorpeen. Extremely deadly. "

"It looks like a tobacco hornworm," Smoke remarked. "Just ten times uglier."

The vorpeen came right at them.

Smoke and Sid fired. Bullets ripped through the beast's body. It reared up on its thousands of back legs, squealing an ear-splitting shriek. "EeeEEEeeeeeEEeeeee!"

Covering his ears, Vormus yelled, "Don't shoot it! It will only attract more. They aren't easy to kill."

Sid figured that out soon enough. The vorpeen advanced. Sid shot it in the face.

Blam! Blam!

Its bullet wounds oozed. It stopped coming. Its body twisted and writhed.

"I said not to shoot it," Vormus said with disappointment. "They come."

Three more vorpeens appeared from the darkness. The silent things crept right at them with their horns lowered. Their pinchers clacked.

Aiming from one vorpeen to the other, Sid said, "So how are we supposed to kill them?"

"You don't. You run from them. They'll just keep coming unless they're fed."

Sid and Smoke's gunfire echoed in the chamber like the sound of a raging thunderstorm.

The vorpeens wriggled and squirmed. Their guts splashed the cavern floor.

"Looks like they die to me," Smoke said. "And I've got plenty of bullets. How many can there be?"

With anger in his voice, Vormus said, "How many bees are in a hive?"

Three vorpeens became six.

Sid and Smoke looked at one another and said simultaneously, "Elevator!"

Backing away from the monstrous bugs, she took a glance over her shoulder. Eugene the Toad Man stood in the elevator with a broad smile on his face. He smiled and waved. "Goodbye, mortals!" The doors started to close.

"Wait!" Sid screamed.

Smoke turned just as the doors clicked shut. "That sucks."

CHAPTER 8

V ORMUS FLOATED UP OFF THE floor.

Still shooting the monsters, Sid said, "You get down here and fight!"

"I didn't start this fight. Besides, I don't want to get my sweater dirty." He picked off a fragment of debris from his shoulder. "I'm rather fond of it."

She pointed the Glock at him. "Get down here and fight, or I'm gonna shoot you!"

A knot of centipedes stormed her feet, at least a hundred pounds of them. It made her skin crawl. She sent two bullets through one's face. The blue-tipped rounds ripped the back of its head out. The second vorpeen devoured the first. The third one kept coming.

"Crap! Smoke, I'm down to the red tip!" She popped out one clip and exchanged it for another. Suddenly, a sea of vorpeens appeared by the dozens, snapping at her legs with pinchers. She blasted off round after round. "I'm going to run out of ammo."

"I knew I should have brought a machine gun." Firing

with two hands, Smoke cracked off shot after shot. The bugs piled up in heaps.

It wasn't enough. Within seconds, they were surrounded by the vermin again. Pinchers fastened on Sid's leg and held her tight. She screamed, "Aaaaaaarrgh!" She fired. *Blam!*

The entire chamber became a bug bath. The wriggling masses devoured their own dead, filling their mouths with their brethren's flesh. The insects came *en masse* at Smoke and Sid.

Covered in gore and sweat, she fought the masses. They tangled her ankles and crawled up her spine. She grabbed one by the neck, slung it through the air, and shot it.

Out of nowhere, Smoke appeared. He ripped the bugs away from her ankles, tearing them apart with his hands. "They squish," he said. A bug crawled up his shoulder. He grabbed its pinchers and ripped them apart. "I bet these would make great bait for really big fish."

"Too bad we aren't hunting whale today," she said.

"Maybe tomorrow."

"Ugh!" She kicked another vorpeen free, then stomped its head under her heel. "Can't you regurgitate some bug repellent or something?" She sprinted by the next wave of bugs and jumped up on a desk. "Vormus! Get the elevator back!"

The vorpeens didn't chase after Vormus. He had a clear path to the elevator. He floated over and pushed the button. "You see? I helped, but I don't think anything is coming. You know, it's the blood they so enjoy. If you were immortal like me, it wouldn't be a problem."

"Shut up!" Sid shot another and another.

Fighting at her side, Smoke said, "I have an idea. Vormus, did you say they were coming out of a cave back there?"

"I don't see them coming from anywhere else."

Smoke snatched Sid's clip that held one red bullet. He winked at her. "I'll be back." He ran through the field of centipedes.

Fighting the centipedes, she watched him disappear. Within moments, gunfire cracked off in the blackness, followed by loud booms. The floor shook. A billowing dust cloud spilled out of the darkness.

"Smoke!" she screamed as she fought.

The rangy man emerged from the hazy mist. He killed everything crawly in sight, working his way back to Sid. "I think a cave-in might hold them."

At a furious pace, they fought off every last vorpeen until they were all dead. No more came. Coated in bug splatter, he said to Sid, "Did you use a vitamin?"

"No. You?"

He shook his head. Surveying all the mutilated bugs, he said, "That was awesome."

Sid turned. "Vormus, is the elevator back?"

"No." He applauded them with a gentle clap. "Marvelous work, but I think we have another problem."

"What's that?"

The block walls cracked. Water squirted through. The lights quavered again.

"This place is going to collapse at any moment."

CHAPTER 9

T HEY'VE BEEN IN THERE TOO long," Sam said
to Guppy. They stood outside, leaning on
Guppy's truck. He held some binoculars to
his eyes. A fog had covered Fort Carroll in a hazy mist.
The outline of the island could barely be seen. "I knew
we should have brought a boat."

"It's barely been an hour," Guppy said. "They're
usually gone much longer than that."

Looking down at her husband, the high-heeled
woman took away his binoculars. "Excuse me, honey?"

"Er…I can swim over and check on them if you like."

"I might just have you do that." Her long nails dug
into her hands. "Aw, I'm sorry, hon. You know I hate
waiting. I have a bad feeling, too. Something just doesn't
seem right."

"The fog and the moon don't help much either. They
bring the stink of the supernatural. They'll be back soon.
I'm sure of it."

Sam sent a text to Sid. Her painted eyes were intent
on the screen. "They've gone dark, all right."

The ground shook under her feet.

Sam's body straightened. "Did you feel that?"

"I sure did." Guppy glanced at the ground. "That was weird."

"What the hell was it?"

He shrugged his brawny shoulders.

"They don't have earthquakes in DC, do they?" she asked.

"Not that I remember." He scanned the traffic zooming by on the Francis Scott Key Bridge. "I don't see or hear any big trucks that could have moved the ground like that. It felt like the ground farted."

Sam pinched her nose. "Or maybe you did? You didn't, did you?"

"No, no, honey, it wasn't me."

She eyed him.

"I swear."

"At least we're outside." In the corner of her eye, she saw someone moving through the fog. She hit guppy in the arm and pointed.

A man approached, dripping from head to toe. He wore nothing but a pair of jeans. The rest of the stocky figure was difficult to see in the fog and darkness. His attention was elsewhere when he noticed Sid's car. He stopped and looked.

Guppy reached inside his truck and grabbed a shotgun then eased in front of Sam. She drew her nickel-plated 1911 semi-auto from her belt. It had pink pearl grips. Together, they approached. Guppy charged the pump on the shotgun. It caught the man's attention. He stepped full into the light.

Sam made a face like she had swallowed a bug. The squat, dripping-wet guy hunkered down on his thick legs. His skin was toady. His hands and feet were webbed. His huge eyes bulged from the sockets.

"Good evening," he said. His long tongue licked out, snatching a bug. He sucked it back in between his thin lips. "Is this your car? It's a fine machine."

Nerves tingling and skin crawling, Sam said, "Get away from the car, frog lips." She charged the slide on her weapon. Trembling a little, she pointed the weapon at him. "Or I'll blow your warts off."

"Heh." The Toad Man lifted his webbed hands. There were pronounced claws on them. A sliver of a smile crossed his fat face. "I'm not a frog but a toad. Toad Man, they call me. Humph. I suppose you're with those other clowns who sought to detain me. How humorous." His bulging eyes blinked. "They are dead."

"You're lying," Sam said.

"No. They're finished. Soon, you will be too." Toad Man gave Sam a lusty once-over. "I might keep you alive for a bit. You are a feast for the eyes. It's been a long, long time since I've shared company with a woman." He took a step forward.

"That's not going to happen, tadpole," Guppy said. "One more step and I'll scatter your guts all over this place."

"Hah. Your friends' weapons didn't work on me. Your weapons can't harm me either, mortals. What's your name, pretty lady? I'm Eugene 'Toad Man' Green. And you are?"

"Not interested." Sam squeezed the trigger.

Toad Man sprang over both of them.

She turned. Toad Man was gone. "Where'd he go?"

"Not sure," Guppy said.

Hands beat on the hood of Guppy's truck. It was Toad Man. He laughed.

Sam and Guppy took aim.

Toad Man vanished. His laughter carried in the night. From out in the darkness, he said, "I hate mortals. I enjoy killing them one at a time."

"Stay close, Sam," Guppy said.

"I will." Her heart pounded in her chest. She stood back to back with Guppy. Together they turned slowly, searching all around. Something bounded across her path and vanished. "He's so fast."

Toad Man cackled. "You have no idea, dear."

A rock skipped over the pavement. It cracked Sam in the ankle. "Gah!" She fell to the ground, clutching her leg. Tears watered her eyes. "Man, that hurt!"

Shotgun low and eyes wary, Guppy crouched over her. "I'll find him. Hang in there."

Sam didn't see any sign of the man anywhere. She looked in all directions. "I don't see him."

With a wild-eyed look, Toad Man dropped out of the darkness right behind Guppy. His clawed hands locked on Guppy's shoulders. He slung the burly man aside like a small child, smashing Guppy into the truck's quarter panel.

Guppy lay still.

Sam took aim.

Toad Man swatted the gun from her hand with alarming force. He licked his lips. "You're mine now, pretty lady."

CHAPTER 10

WATER POURED THROUGH THE WALL of the cavern like it would through a huge crack in the Hoover Dam. It was up to Sid's knees and rising fast. The vorpeen floated among the inner tide, splashing in the surge. The ones that still lived wrestled with their fate. Sid was glad. It appeared the vorpeen couldn't swim. It was a small victory.

"Smoke, how are we going to get out of here?" she demanded.

The rangy man's hands were digging into the slit between the elevator doors. His face filled with strain. "Man, these doors are stubborn!"

Sid sloshed through the waters. She grabbed hold from the other side. The doors wouldn't move. The lights quavered in and out. The darkness came and went like the door of a coffin opening and closing. She glanced up at Vormus, who floated just beneath the ceiling. "A little help?"

Frowning, he said, "I'm not fond of getting wet."

"You're going to get wet one way or the other. Now get your ass down here!"

Vormus complied, sinking in the air and landing beside Sid. She stepped aside. The shifter sank his nails into the crack between the doors. He eyed Smoke.

"On three," Smoke said. "Three!" Putting all his muscle into it, he grunted. His face filled with strain.

A notable amount of concentration formed on Vormus's pale face.

The elevator doors parted a foot with a groan, revealing emptiness. No elevator.

Sid jumped into action. She wedged her body inside the seam and pushed with her knee. While water spilled into the elevator shaft, she pushed with all her strength. There was a pop. The metal doors gave way. "We need to climb," she said.

Smoke nodded.

Vormus slipped inside the shaft and floated up, saying, "I'd carry you if I could, but my power is limited. Good luck." He vanished up into the pitch-black shaft.

"Over here," Smoke said. The water was up to his chest. His hand locked on an emergency ladder built into the shaft. He grabbed Sid by the hand and pulled her over. "You go first."

Hand over hand, she raced up the ladder. In the black, she could no longer see a thing. It was like climbing inside a tunnel with no end. The water rose under them, trying to swallow them whole. Sid felt like the entire island was sinking.

"Hurry, Sid," Smoke said.

Fueled by adrenaline, she climbed. It seemed to never

end. One rung after another, she hoped to see a glimmer of light. She hollered up the shaft, "Vormus?"

There was no reply.

Panic set in. She didn't have any idea how deep the shaft was to begin with. The elevator ride had been so long. Her limbs grew tired. They'd just battled countless vorpeen to the point of exhaustion. Now she was fighting for her life again. And at the top, she knew the elevator would be blocking their way out. Another enemy to fight in the pitch black. "Smoke, how deep are we?"

"I don't know, but the water is almost on my toes. Keep moving!"

She stopped. "I'm not going out like this without a fight." She dug out her supervitamin pill, stuck it in her mouth, bit down, and swallowed. She resumed the climb. The higher she went, the more her shoulders ached. At last, the pill kicked in and the throbbing eased. She climbed faster. "Vormus, where are you?"

The shifter shouted back, "Under this albatross of an elevator."

Sid practically ran up the ladder. Her head smote a metal beam. She shook it off. She could sense Vormus. The vitamin enhanced her sight just enough to make out an outline of the shifter above. "Get out of the way."

Vormus drifted aside.

Holding onto the rung by one hand, she leaned over and punched the bottom of the elevator with the other.

"Heavens, what are you doing?" Vormus asked.

"I'm getting us out of here!" She cocked back and punched again. *Wham!* Hitting the metal over and over, she found a soft spot in the floor. She punched several times. It wouldn't give.

"Sid, the water's rising fast," Smoke said.

"I know that!" She laid into it with everything she had. The water was still flooding the shaft. She took a breath. They were all underwater now. She lost the force she needed to put behind her swing. Her fingers found the edge of the metal panel.

Please, Jesus, don't let us die like this!

She began peeling it back. More strong fingers joined hers. With a wrench and a heave, the panel peeled away. Sid shoved herself up and burst through the elevator's flooring. She grabbed Smoke's arm and pulled him through. Smoke did the same for Vormus. All together, they pulled open the elevator doors. The three of them spilled out into the tunnel under the forest. The water spilled out, too, and vanished through a grate in the floor. Sid coughed and gasped for air. Smoke and Vormus did the same.

Sucking for air, Smoke said, "That was close. Nice job, honey. How's your hand?"

Still filled with energy, she opened and closed her fingers. "Well, there's probably going to be some swelling." She grabbed Smoke's hand with her other one, and the two of them helped each other to their feet. "Come on."

With some feeble coughing, Vormus fell in behind them, and on their way out of the tunnel, he said, "Assuming Toad Man was the rat, I can only imagine that within minutes, Kane will know we're coming after him."

Sid was climbing the steps to the topside. "I'm pretty sure he knew that. Why else would he have moved the prisoners? The entire thing was a trap. They knew we'd go in there."

"And to think they almost got all three of us at once." Vormus toyed with the hem of his sweater. "Oh dear, I have a snag."

"It's possible there is a rat among us," Smoke said. He led the way back to their gear. "Either that, or we missed something."

Sid got her phone and texted Sam. "We're out. All is well. Be alert." She didn't get a reply. Sam always replied within seconds. "Something's wrong."

"Why do you say that?"

Sid lurched up. Her enhanced senses picked up a blood-curdling scream in the air.

CHAPTER 11

S UCH A PRETTY FACE. IT'S almost sad to see it go to waste." Toad Man had Sam by the neck. His tongue licked her skin. "Mm, you taste good."

Sam punched him in the groin.

The shifter didn't flinch. "Really? Have you any idea how many times that's happened?"

She drew back and hit him again.

His eyelids flicked up.

"That's two times I know of, tadpole."

A heavy force collided with Toad Man. It tore his grip from Sam.

Guppy had his powerful arms locked around Toad Man's head. He scissor locked Toad Man's legs with his own legs. Face reddening, he held onto Toad Man. The silent ball of muscles did everything in his power to crush the life out of the shifter.

The supernaturally powered shifter shed the burly man. He pummeled Guppy in the face several times.

Guppy staggered back on wobbling legs. His nose was bleeding. He steadied himself and advanced.

"Oh, so pathetic. Brave mortals so eager to test their mortality. It's no wonder the Drake finds them so entertaining." Toad Man set his shoulders. "Come on then. I like the screams that come when I break bones."

"Hey wart-face." Sam stood behind him with the shotgun. "You forgot somebody."

"Oh, how dreary." He spread out his arms. "Fine, shoot me with your little shotgun. I could use the tickle." He scratched his shoulder with his webbed fingers and claws. "As a matter of fact, I have an itch right here."

She squeezed the trigger. With a *pow*, a net made of metal webbing burst from the barrel. Expanding in an instant, the net covered Toad Man from head to toe. The links engulfed his body and wrapped him up from side to side.

Toad Man gaped. "What the hell is this?" He struggled against the bonds. The more he wiggled, the tighter the net became.

"It's called a toad catcher," Guppy said. He marched over and slugged Toad Man in the belly. "That's for touching Sam." He pushed the shifter to the ground and kicked him repeatedly in the ribs. "This is for all those others you killed, murderous fiend!"

A boat skidded up the boat ramp. Sid and Smoke jumped out and rushed over. "Oh my, you got him!" Sid said with a wild look in her eye. "I can't believe it." She hugged Sam. "Thank God you're safe."

"It was nothing," Sam said. "I just hope he doesn't give me warts. If I get a wart, I'll kill him myself."

"We can't be killed, mortal!" Toad Man yelled.

Vormus floated down to the ground. "On the contrary, there are plenty of ways to kill a shifter. Totally destroying the body is one. That's going to happen to you, Eugene." Lording over the man, he added, "I suggest you cooperate."

"Never. You know as I do you can't defeat Kane and his minions."

"His thick skin is thinner when the sun is up. I'm sure he'll be more willing to talk then."

Sirens and lights were racing across the Francis Scott Key Bridge.

"Time to go," Smoke said. "Pop the trunk, Sam."

The back lid of the Hellcat opened.

Smoke picked Eugene up by the net, dropped him inside, and shut the trunk lid. Sam tossed him the keys. He snatched them out of thin air then glanced at Sid. "Care if I drive?"

Her head was swimming. The vitamin had worn off. "Go for it."

CHAPTER 12

S MOKE PARKED THE HELLCAT BEHIND an old strip mall in a bad neighborhood. Graffiti covered the exterior walls. Train tracks ran behind him. He got out of the car. Sid and Vormus joined him. Sam and Guppy hadn't followed. They'd set out on another mission.

Facing a metal door, he pressed the button on the side then glanced up at the camera overhead. Moments later, the door popped open and a little head appeared around the door's edge. It was Asia. "Aw shit, it's you."

"Good to see you too, Asia," Smoke said. "Is Mal in?"

"No. Goodbye." She tried to close the door.

Smoke held the door fast. "After you, Sid."

Sid shoved by Asia.

"Watch where you're going, hippopotamus!" Asia said with her usual disdain, but then she got her first look at Vormus and snarled, "What the hell are you?"

"A vampire."

She fixed her slanted stare on his chest. "Very ugly sweater. And why are you all wet?"

"Hold the door," Smoke said to Vormus. He fetched Eugene out of the trunk and hauled him inside.

"What the hell is that?" Asia fanned her nose. "And why do you all smell like the river? Mal! Mal! Your spooky friends have returned. They smell like bad sushi!" In her bright-orange kimono, she hustled away. "Mal! Take care of your visitors. I'm finishing *The Young and the Restless*."

The strip mall had a sublevel to it. The walls were concrete like an unfinished basement. The lighting was all fluorescent. It was filled with a bunch of secondhand furniture consisting of a king-size bed, sofas, tables, and several desks. Mal sat in front of a wall of monitors with active images on all the screens. The scholarly man wore a rumpled lab coat. His hair was long and frazzled. He looked like he hadn't shaved in days. He clicked on the mouse.

Sid slumped on the couch. Her head was leaned back in the cushions. She could barely keep her eyes open. She'd never felt so exhausted before. It was like she had just swum the English Channel—not once but twice.

Smoke was talking. His voice was low and soothing. He caught Mal up on everything from the time Vormus came up until right now. Eugene Green lay on the floor, huddled up and whining.

It was morning.

Toad Man was all man. The net was off. He was secured by two sets of flex cuffs that bound his wrists and ankles. He had griped when Asia applied the cuffs.

She'd smacked him in the back of the head, saying, "Shut up or I'll chicken fry your frog legs, ugly man."

Mal's body language didn't sit well with Sid. He was a little bit out of it. She leaned forward and gave Asia a nod.

Asia shuffled over and leaned down. "What?"

"Is Mal okay?"

"He's never been all right. We used to make love three times a day, and now it's barely three times a month."

"That's not what I meant." Sid pulled at her imaginary beard. "Why's he so shaggy?"

"What do you expect? We're living in a strip mall. There isn't even a shower. I have to go to the YMCA and take a shower after I work out. All the round eyes are always staring at me. Burly men." Her face soured. "I don't like them. I like them scrawny myself. Except Smoke." She eyed the dark and handsome man. "He's a fine specimen. How many times a day do you two—"

"Is Mal sick?"

Asia popped back. "No. Not sick. Just goofy. I have to go." She hustled out the door and upstairs.

Sid found Smoke looking back at her. She could tell he had heard what she said. That was when she heard Mal speak out loud for the first time. "I am sick, Sidney, but it will pass." He turned around in his chair and let out a rough cough. "Asia says I'm not taking enough vitamins and I work too hard. Both are true."

"Me and Vormus know a cure for that," Eugene said. He sat on the floor, straining against his bonds. "Though I don't think they'd take the likes of you, professor."

Vormus swatted Eugene in the back of the head so

hard his chin hit his chest. "Be silent, fool. I'm close enough to ripping you apart that one wrong syllable will trigger me."

Eugene clammed up. His eyes attached themselves to the floor.

"We need more information from him," Smoke said to Mal. "He's not talking. You got anything for that?"

Mal lifted a brow. "So, you want to use a truth serum on a shifter? I've never tried before. Humph. I'd be delighted."

"Let's get to it then," Smoke said.

"Eh, the problem is I don't have one. I'm not the CIA, you know."

Smoke pushed the sleeves of the sweetheart suit up to his elbows. The muscles rippled in his forearms. "I guess we'll have to do this the hard way then."

"What hard way?" Sid asked.

"Torture."

"Do you even know how to torture a shifter?" Eugene said, choking out a laugh. "What are you going to do, waterboard me? I'm more amphibian than man. I can take all the pain you can dish out."

Walking over, Smoke stooped above the shifter. "So it won't bother you if I push your eyes back into your head?"

Eugene swallowed. "Er…no?"

"Don't fret, everyone." Mal forced himself out of his chair and sauntered over to a lab table. He opened up an alligator-skin doctor's bag and dug out a metal case. Unclipping the hasp, he opened it up. There was a vial and a syringe inside. "This poison may or may not kill him, but he's going to feel like he's had a heart attack at least a dozen times." He filled the syringe with the clear contents of the vial. "Should I do the honors or should you, Smoke?"

"Vormus, help me hold him." Smoke said, taking Eugene by the arm.

"Disappointing," said the vampire. "I wanted to see you push his bulbous eyes back inside his head. Honestly, I can take care of this dilemma myself."

"You didn't do so well back in the fort."

"His bluff fooled us all." Vormus held the shifter fast. "It happens."

Mal sank the needle into the shifter's neck.

Eugene screamed.

CHAPTER 13

EUGENE'S EYES BECAME FEVERISH. THEY darted from face to face. "What did you do?" he shrieked desperately. "What have you done to me?"

"Does it burn?" Mal said, tapping the syringe. "Hmmm, I accidently took some of his fluids out, which could be helpful for my research."

Smoke took out his knife and held the blade in Eugene's face. "I could take some skin from him. It'll grow back. I think toad DNA heals up. Isn't that what they used in the first Hulk movie?"

"No, that was *Jurassic Park*," Mal corrected.

"Actually, they used frog DNA in both of them," Sid added.

Smoke gave her a nod.

Mal checked his watch. "Eugene Green, is it?"

The shifter licked his lips between shudders and gasps. "Yes, Eugene Green."

"Those severe heart palpitations should start up any moment," said Mal. "Just remember, it will go on for hours. Your chest will feel like it's caving in on itself, like an earthquake inside your frame, but I have an antidote." He fished through the doctor's bag. "At least I use to have one. Oh crap, I'll be right back."

"What?" Eugene lurched up. "Where's he going?"

"Just sit back, Eugene. He'll be back." Smoke talked nice and easy. "Mal's not one to lose things. Besides, you're tough. A few heart attacks will feel like a walk in the park for a tough guy like you. Say, where would a guy like you be from, anyway? I'm guessing Jersey. Are you a Jersey boy, Eugene? Where are you from?"

"I'm from King of Prussia near Philly."

Sid eased over.

Smoke gave Sid an approving glance. He continued. "I've been there before. Nice place. They have a pretty big shopping mall there, don't they?"

"Yes. But that's well after my time." Eugene strained his neck. Peering at the stairs, he said, "Where is he with the antidote? I feel like my heart is pounding out my ears."

"He'll be back. Do you want a drink?" Smoke asked.

"Yes."

"Good. Sid, will you check the fridge over there?"

"Right away."

Eugene shuddered. Wide eyed, he stared at Smoke. "Where is he with the antidote?"

"Hmmm, it looks like the travails are just beginning. That was a pretty bad tremor. Your teeth clacked. Uh," Smoke looked around, "we might want to get him something to bite down on."

Vormus handed Smoke a pencil. "Here."

"I was thinking something more substantial."

Sid returned with a can of Coke. She cracked it open. "Do you like Coke?"

"I once did." He took a sip. "Where's the antidote?" Eugene's eyes were all over the place.

Sid took a seat in front of the computer monitors.

Smoke asked Eugene, "Where can we find Manson Bay?"

"145 Allen Towers."

Sid typed it in. A picture popped up on the screen next to a map, the gate of a condominium duplex community west of DC as one headed toward the West Virginia border.

"Where did Kane take all the shifters?"

"Drake Headquarters." Eugene jerked in his bonds. He slobbered. "Where's the antidote?"

"It's coming." Smoke said. "Where's Drake Headquarters?"

"Near Hillcrest Mausoleum."

"What are Kane's big plans?"

"He wants to replace Washington leadership with clones. He wants to capture you and Sid. He wants domination over the world."

"Does he have Allison and Megan with him?"

"I don't know. But they will change if they haven't already. Where's the antidote?"

Sid typed up everything he mentioned, in a message to Sam and Guppy. They'd start pulling up all the information they could find.

Vormus had a question. "Manson Bay—was he in the prison very long?"

"No, he was never there when I was there."

"Why'd they all leave?"
"They knew you were coming."
"How did they know we were coming?"
"Because someone in your group is a clone."

CHAPTER 14

S ID'S HEART SKIPPED A BEAT. Her fatigue evaporated
when Eugene said what he said. It was entirely
possible one of them was a traitor. It was the only
way.

The next question Smoke asked was the obvious one.
"Which one of us is the clone?"

"I don't know. Where's the antidote?"

Mal came down the steps and entered the basement
room. "Oh dear me, as it turns out, there isn't an antidote
after all."

"What!" Eugene's husky neck bulged. "What do you
mean?"

"How did our session go?" Mal asked Smoke.

"I think we have everything we need. He did admit
one thing I didn't expect. He says one of us is a clone."

"Really?" Mal adjusted his glasses. "Which one?"

"He doesn't know."

"I don't have much of a lab set up here, but I'm
certain we could run a test."

"We don't have time for that now."

"Hold on," Eugene interrupted. "You say there's no antidote?"

"No, you don't need one. I injected you with a truth serum. It will wear off."

"But you said you didn't have the truth serum," Eugene said.

"I know. I lied." Mal took an open chair in front of the monitors. His fingers got busy on the keyboards. "I'll see what I can find. In the meantime, what are we going to do with him? Or it, rather?"

"We can't count on the FBI anymore. It would be another catch and release. We could leave him here," Sid suggested.

"This isn't a prison. We aren't equipped to handle him." Mal shrugged. "I bet your new pal Vormus has an idea."

"It would be best to kill him. Just let me handle it." The vampire shifter pulled Toad Man up by his hair. "I can see to it he never returns again."

"Killing is not an ideal way to restore your humanity," said Sid.

"No, but just think how many lives I will save. But if you insist, I'll let him live. Live in misery."

"Screw it. Just stick him back in the trunk. We'll take him with us." Smoke glanced at Mal. "We're going to need all the supplies you have if we're going to take these shifters out. They've freed all the ones we caught before."

"Give me a few days," Mal replied.

"We'll be in touch," Smoke said. "And see what you can whip up in regards to a DNA test. If one of us is a clone, the sooner we know, the better."

"I'm working on it as we speak. Chow."

They left the building and stuck Eugene in the trunk. Vormus faced both of them. "I'm going after Manson Bay."

"No," Sid objected. "You're staying with us."

"Hardly." Vormus's feet left the ground. Up in the sky he went. "I'll be in touch."

"Do you get the feeling we aren't any closer than we were before?" she asked.

"Uh-huh." Smoke cupped her cheek in his hand. "How are you feeling?"

"I'm not going to lie, I could use some sleep. So, do you really think one of us is a clone? Sam or Guppy? You'd think we could tell."

"True. What did you think about Mal?"

"He's off."

Smoke opened up her door. "I thought so too."

CHAPTER 15

"WELCOME HOME, EUGENE," SMOKE SAID. He opened up a single-car garage in an old neighborhood. The brick garage was at the bottom of an old abandoned colonial house that was deteriorating. Heavy growth covered the front porch. The lawn hadn't been cut in years. The place was spooky.

"You aren't really going to leave me here, are you?" Eugene said.

Smoke pushed the man into the garage. It had one single-pane window, dingy with dirt. Daylight crept in, forming pools of yellow light on the floor. He strapped Eugene to the support beam. He lifted another pair of flex cuffs to Eugene's eyes.

"What are you going to do with those?"

"Seal your mouth shut. Even though we are far from many, I can't afford to have you screaming. Anything else you'd like to tell us before we leave?"

Turning his chin away, Eugene said, "No."

"Good." Smoke secured the shifter's mouth with the flex cuffs. He tested all the bonds to make sure they were secure. Once he finished, he took out his phone and took some pictures of Eugene. "I don't think the Drake is going to be very happy when we let them know you told us everything. You say you can't be killed, but I'm pretty sure shifters know how to kill shifters."

Toad Man slumped to the floor.

Smoke took one last glance around the garage. He stepped outside, where Sidney waited, and closed the door. He locked it shut. "Ready to go?"

Yawning, she said, "Ready as ever."

They got in the car and took off. Smoke drove. Sid leaned her seat back and closed her eyes. They were miles out of DC on some back roads that didn't have much traffic. "So whose property was that?"

"That's one of the hideouts of some marks I tracked down years ago. Last I checked, they were still in prison."

"You keep tabs on them?"

"Yep."

Sid shifted in her seat. "I can't wait to take a shower. This second skin is starting to stink."

"We're going home, but I have to make a stop first."

"Milkshake run?"

Smoke smiled.

"I knew it," she said. With her hand on her stomach, she said, "I think I could use one too. I'm starving." Fighting the sleep that was wanting to take over, she said, "What's the plan?"

"As much as I hate to say it, I think you and I might need to go it alone for a bit. We have the addresses. We just need to do our thing until we figure out who is who."

"So you don't think I'm a clone? I could be Samone."

"No, you aren't her. She wasn't nearly as pretty. Besides, she had a unibrow. I just didn't make the connection until it was too late."

Sid burst out laughing.

"I thought it was a new trend or something. Like the Europeans. She had a moustache coming in too."

Still laughing, she hit him in the arm. "Stop it. I can't take anymore. I'm too tired to laugh."

Smoke grinned. He hit the interstate ramp and gunned the gas, accelerating long enough to merge with the morning traffic. "Great Dane. So, Sid, do you think I'm a clone?"

"No, but the thought of two of you is pretty intriguing."

"How so?"

With a little smile on her lips, she shrugged. "It just is."

"Sounds like somebody needs a cold shower."

"And a hot man. Sorry, I'm so tired I'm feeling giddy."

"That's fine by me. After all, you are my wife."

It took an hour to get to Smoke and Sid's garage apartment. Together, they hit the shower and went to bed.

Sid woke up in the early evening. Her stomach was queasy. She padded over to the bathroom on bare feet and closed the door. She leaned over the sink and stared into the mirror. Her eyes were tired. "I need to get more rest. I feel like I've been up for days." She rinsed off her face with some cold water. Her stomach quavered. She patted her face dry with a towel and sauntered out of the bathroom as quietly as she could.

Smoke was up. He stood in the kitchenette brewing coffee. Eyeing her, he said, "Are you okay?"

Pushing her hair back, she replied, "Don't I look okay?"

"You always look okay, but you're a little peaked." He filled the coffee pot with water, stuck it in the coffee maker, and flipped the switch. He walked up to Sid. Placing the back of his hand on her forehead, he said, "You don't feel hot."

"Gee, thanks, Mom." She brushed his hand aside. "I'll be fine once I get some caffeine back in my system. That vitamin really took it out of me."

"How's your hand?"

She lifted her fist. Her knuckles were swollen and scraped. Clutching her fingers in and out, she said, "Maybe a hairline fracture is causing my queasiness. Lord, I hope not. I need my shooting hand."

With a furrowed brow, Smoke said, "Maybe you need to check in with a doctor. When's the last time you had a physical?"

"Now I'm starting to think you *are* a clone. Are you seriously suggesting I visit some—as you like to put it—overeducated quack?"

"I know a guy."

"Of course you do." She patted his chest and made her way toward the coffee. The rich aroma aroused her senses. "Yesterday was quite a day. Not to mention the extended nocturnal activities. No, I'll be fine."

A glare shined into the kitchen window. Outside, a rubber tire screeched.

Smoke pushed the curtain aside.

An SUV sped toward the building, swerving from side to side.

Smoke snatched a shotgun and rushed out the front door. He took aim at the oncoming car. He fired one shot in the air. The car skidded to a halt. It was a banged-up white SUV. Someone slumped over the wheel. It was Vormus.

CHAPTER 16

S MOKE OPENED THE CAR DOOR. Vormus fell into his arms. The disheveled vampire shifter's clothing was torn to shreds. His face was bruised and swollen. "What happened to you?"

Barely able to stand, Vormus pointed over his shoulder. "Get him out. Get him out."

Gun in hand, Sid flung open the back door.

A little olive-skinned boy was buckled in the back seat. He appeared about ten years old. He wore a blue suit and necktie. His hair was gray and hung over his eyes. His mouth and arms were tied up.

Vormus's exposed skin sizzled in the sun. He staggered under the garage apartment's canopy and inside the building.

"Smoke, he's got a kid in here," she said, unbuckling the boy's belt.

From inside the apartment, Vormus said, "He's not a child. He's much older than I. Bring him inside."

Sid scooped the boy up in her arms. She took him inside and set him on the couch.

Vormus leaned against the kitchen counter. Dabbing his forehead with a silk handkerchief, he said, "I never thought daylight would be my ally."

"What's going on, Vormus?" Sid started tearing the tape away from the boy's mouth. "You're kidnapping children now?"

"I wouldn't do that. Again, he's no child. He is Manson Bay, the keeper of secrets. He's far from harmless."

Smoke entered the room and closed the door behind him. He said to Vormus, "So, who got the best of you?"

"The deaders. Not to mention Titus Tolliver."

"The gargoyle?" Sid said.

"Yes. Kane keeps Manson under a heavy watch. Manson is notorious for giving Kane the slip." Vormus rubbed his jaw. "That's why I thought he'd be in Fort Carroll. The little trickster would be secure there."

Manson's eyes were like black soul-searching pearls. They searched every inch of Sid's face. The boy's body was clearly controlled by an intelligence far beyond his appearance.

"So what do we need him for?" Sid asked. "What kind of secrets does he keep?"

"Manson knows the cures. Not just for me but for your sister."

"You say that as if she's already been changed."

With his eyes glued on Sid, Manson nodded. It sent chills through her.

"I thought you said they were going to change her, not that she'd changed!" She stormed over to Vormus. "How do you know this?"

"Manson told me."

71

"And how does he know everything?"

"Because he is the one in charge of the process. He converted your sister from a mortal to a shifter."

Sid slapped Vormus across the jaw. "Don't say that! Don't lie!"

Smoke moved between the two. "You said she'd have to kill someone first, right, Vormus? A loved one? Only then would the process be complete."

"Why are you asking him?" Sid moved over to Manson. "Let's just ask this little twerp." She finished ripping the tape from his mouth. "Out with it, Manson!"

"Ow!" Manson cried out. "Geez, woman, go easy on an old man." The child spoke as if he was a venerable eighty. "I'm all wrinkly inside, and I don't feel anything like I look on the outside. Don't let the appearance fool you. Heh."

"You're a shifter. Shifters don't age."

"No, that's where you're wrong, we do age. The process is just slow. Everything on earth deteriorates. It's the second law of thermodynamics. That's what shifters refuse to understand. They think they are immortal, but they are not." He glanced at his surroundings. "You look like a reasonable, very fit, and attractive woman. I need to pee." His brows clenched. "I'm at the point where it's painful."

"Vormus?"

The elegant shifter shrugged. "He's harmless from a physical standpoint."

"Then why did you tie him up?"

"I've kidnapped many. It's always best to tether them with something."

Sid unfastened the tiny man's bonds and led him to the bathroom. Leaving the door open, she said, "Make it quick."

"I certainly don't have any desire for it to take any longer than it has to." He pushed the door shut. "A little privacy, please."

"Vormus?"

"He's harmless."

She moved away from the door. "I don't believe that. He's a shifter, isn't he?"

"Point taken. But he's mild mannered. You'll see."

The commode flushed. The bathroom sink water ran. The door opened, and Manson came out. He wasn't the same olive-skinned boy as before. Now he had a full head of straight blond hair and blue eyes. A quizzical look was on his face. "Ah, now I feel much better." The boyish figure walked like he was in his seventies. He tried to climb on a stool by Vormus. "A little help."

Smoke gave him a boost into the chair.

Manson felt Smoke's bicep. "See, I'll never have those. Sad, isn't it? This body never even hit puberty, but my mind sure did. I've been like this since the eleventh century—you know, when King Arthur and Lancelot were around." He winked at Sid. "I bet you thought that was only a legend, didn't you?"

"Thanks for the info, Benjamin Button, but I never gave it a shred of thought."

He shrugged. "Do you have any tea?"

"In a minute. Tell me about my sister."

"Oh, Allison. Boy, that woman's trouble. She's side by side with Kane day and night. He's not letting her or

Megan out of his sight. They're the bait. He's patient. He knows you'll come. That's why he let all the shifters out. He's not taking any chances when you guys come around again. Nope. He's sinister. He always has been, but today, boy, you really screwed up his plans."

"What do you mean?" Sid reached into the cupboard and grabbed a box of tea bags.

"Well, now you have me. I'm his prized possession. You see, now I'm the bait, and he will come after me." He leaned over to Vormus. "Haven't you told them that once the sun drops, he'll be coming?"

"I haven't had the chance."

"Vormus, must you always be so contrary?"

"I like contrary. It suits me. Just like this modest establishment suits them."

"Sounds like it's time to gear up," Smoke said. "How many can we expect?"

Manson's eyes widened. "You're not going to wait for them here, are you? It will be a slaughter."

Smoke opened up an army-green footlocker set beside his computer station. Inside were two L.A.W. rockets. He said to Manson, "I'm counting on it."

"You really are crazy, but your maddened bravery won't defeat them." Manson drummed on the counter. "There aren't enough of you. There are plenty of them. You need to hide, at least until daylight. Best to strike in the daytime."

"You know how to stop them, don't you," Sid said. "Tell us."

"Why? That would be to my peril."

Smoke pointed the light antitank weapon at the man. "Not telling us would be to your peril as well."

"Oh, don't be so dramatic."

Smoke tapped on his computer keyboard. "We're set. Let's go."

"Go where?" Vormus asked.

"You'll know when we get there."

CHAPTER 17

S MOKE WAS IN THE PASSENGER seat. Vormus and Manson rode in the back. Sid drove, but her head was swimming with information. She was having trouble keeping track of everything that was going on. Allison may or may not be a shifter. Megan was in danger. At least one of her friends was a clone. All of the shifters they had captured were out loose, and now that night had fallen, they were hunting them. It came down to her and Smoke against a twisted army of fiends. She couldn't even trust her friends in the FBI. And to top everything else off, perhaps she and Smoke were shifters themselves.

Has life always been this insane and I just didn't see it?

She toggled the car's shifter on the wheel, dropping it down a gear. She pushed on the gas, accelerating into the curve.

Vormus squished into Manson.

"Hey, slow it down, will you? I'm not into tasting the G-forces. Get off me, vampire."

"I'll ease off as soon as you start making more sense.

I need to know how to stop Kane. It's time to bring the Drake down."

"Again, you're talking about my life, little lady. I'm not so eager to part with the few remaining years I have left."

"No, but the two of you sound like you seek redemption."

"I'd be lying if I didn't say I'd think about it. Personally, I just want to stick it to Kane. He stuck me in a hole for years. I only got plucked out when he needed me." Manson leaned over the headrest. "Sure, redemption would be nice, but I'm more on the side of vengeance. Personally, Kane is the problem. His ambition overwhelms him. He wants it all at once. You need to take him down if you can."

"That's the plan. But that's only one shifter."

"True, but it will disrupt all the others. A power struggle will ensue. It will buy the mortals more time. At the moment, Kane is replacing leadership with clones. It's weakening our country's policies on many things. Law and order will cease to exist. You'll live in a nation of wild things. But there is a caveat. He has some clones out there, but he can't make any more without me."

"How many clones are out there now?" Sid asked, fearing the answer.

"Dozens." Manson leaned back and peeked out the window. "So, where are we headed?"

"Weapons cache," Smoke said. "I sent a message out to Mal. He sent the coordinates to his latest stockpile. Shipyard. We've got a drive ahead of us. Are you sure you don't have anything you want to fess up? Frankly, I tire of not getting answers to our questions. If the pair of you aren't going to help, then we might as well drop you off right here."

Sid buzzed through a green light in the heart of DC and then parked right in front of the FBI building. She put the car in park and turned around in her seat. "I'm certain the FBI will keep you two fugitives safe."

"You might as well turn us over to Kane," Manson sneered. "Heh, we are fugitives, aren't we." He elbowed Vormus. "Fine. I'll give you something to cut your teeth on then. I know how to kill the clones. One power source controls them all. It works like a server. It's a pyramid, ten feet wide and ten feet tall. It glows with a life of its own. Waters run through it. It's mysticism and technology fused together. It's where the clones are harvested."

"Drake Industries?" Sid asked.

"Hillcrest Mausoleum."

"Just like Toad Man said. We just didn't know what we were looking for."

"What's the security like?" Smoke asked.

"The pea coats are thicker than pea soup," Vormus said.

"So you knew about this?" Sid said.

"No, I know nothing about the clones, but I've been inside that place before, long ago. It's an ordinary building with mortal workers by day, but the shifters guard it by night."

Sid put the car in gear and drove away, headed straight for the shipyard. She shut the engine off as soon as she made it through the gate. Everyone got out of the car.

It was a cargo shipyard. Massive steel storage containers were stacked as far as the eye could see. Smoke led the way with a long, easy stride, pistols nuzzled in his palms. Both he and she had on the sweetheart suits and their goggles.

Smoke checked his phone. His head tilted.

Talking quietly, Sid asked, "What?"

"We're about thirty meters from the mark. We need to keep an eye out and see if anyone else shows up."

"Shifters?"

He shrugged. "If Mal's a clone, then they'll know we're here. That's why I texted him, to draw them out." He scanned the sky. "Who knows? They could come by land, sky, or sea."

"Why don't you go after the weapons cache? You draw them out and I'll back you up?"

"I was thinking about it the other way around, but I'm game." Smoke gave Vormus and Manson a look. Manson turned into a black kid with curly white hair. "What about these two sandbags?"

"They'll just have to stay out of the way," Sid said to the shifters.

"We can help, you know," Vormus said.

"You need to make sure you don't lose Manson. And stay out of the way." Sid motioned Smoke forward with her gun. "Let's go."

Smoke weaved his way through the graveyard of metal shipping containers. Sid stayed one box length away from Smoke, checking high and low. Nothing but them moved or scurried, aside from the soft breeze that kicked up debris from time to time. Smoke came to a stop in front of a blue container sitting by itself beside metal containers stacked four high. He looked all around. His eyes found Sid's.

Sid held up her palm. He waited. She moved quick, scouting the area high and low. She circled the containers and stood face to face with Smoke. "It's all clear. Not a shifter in sight, aside from the two we brought." She rapped her knuckles on the container. "So, this is the one?"

"Yep."

"Well, let's hope Mal is clone free and he's got some nice toys for us." She worked the container's handles. "Still, I hate to think Sam and Guppy are clones. We'd be able to tell, wouldn't we?"

"You'd think." Smoke grabbed the handles and pulled. The doors groaned. Something smashed through the doors, knocking them backward. A wolf man had Smoke pinned down by the throat.

CHAPTER 18

S ID KNEW THE CREATURE INSTANTLY to be Adam Vaughn. The hairy figure was a knot of muscular limbs and power. He wore only a pair of trousers. His savage fury had Smoke flat on the ground. Saliva dripped from the wolf man's jaws. Dazed from having the door smacked into her head, Sid took aim on the wolf man's broad back.

Smoke twisted away from the wolf man in a wrestling move that reversed their positions. Now he had the wolf man on his back.

But in a burst of primal power, the wolf man swatted Smoke aside with his paws. The blow sent Smoke reeling into the container. The wolf man rose, ready to pounce for the kill. He leered at Sid. "You're next, pretty."

She fired several shots. The bullets tore into the wolf man's body.

A.V. staggered back and laughed. "You mortals and your bullets. How pathetic."

"We'll see how you feel about it once I unload this clip into your skull."

"It will be a lesser effect than when I rip your skulls from your heads." A.V. closed in on Smoke.

Sid continued to fire. Regular bullets, unfortunately. They really needed to get to this cache. As A.V. lunged for Smoke, she drew her knife and lunged for A.V.

A shadow dropped from the sky and plowed into her. The blow knocked the knife from her grip. Her head smacked hard into the ground. Shaking it off, she found that a figure loomed over her. It was Angi Harlow, the Night Bird, head to toe in all her feathered glory. The exotic woman was radiant, her smile beautiful and deadly, her eyes cold and merciless.

"We meet again," Angi said. The talons on her feet opened and closed.

Sid drew her other gun and fired.

In a blur of feathers, Night Bird slipped aside. In a moment, she had Sid's hands locked up by the wrists. She squeezed.

Sid gasped. "Ah!" The shifter's grip was iron. She kicked at the feathered woman.

With taloned feet, Night Bird pinned down Sid's legs and pinched her thighs.

She felt the blood stop flowing through them.

"You cannot hurt me, mortal! And I won't underestimate you this time!" Night Bird's face was a mask of anger. "You embarrassed me in my house. In front of my friends. You will pay!" She punched Sid several times with lightning-quick strikes. And then the harpy's wings flapped.

Sid's eyes rolled up in her head. Her body left the ground. Weightlessness overcame her. With blood dripping from her lips and through her swelling eyes, the world below became smaller.

Smoke lay still.

A.V. moved in.

Using his legs, he tripped the wolf man.

The wolf man stumbled.

Smoke struck. He jammed his knife between the shifter's ribs, burying it hilt deep in his heart.

A.V. let out a howl. His arm cocked back. His fist smashed Smoke in the chest with the force of a kicking ram.

Smoke turned aside just enough to evade the full force of the strike. Reeling from the glancing blow, he locked the wolf man's arm up and yanked it out of the socket.

The savage shifter became unglued. The slavering jaws snapped at Smoke's neck. With one arm, he shoved Smoke away. Kicking his elbow back with a pop, A.V. got his shoulder back into place. The hulking brute pulled the knife from his chest and pointed it at Smoke, panting. "That was close. Mortal blades can cut me, but they can't kill me." He eyed the blade in the moonlight. "Ah, but this is special steel. Maybe my claws can't peel the second skin from your limbs, but this can." He showed a fierce smile. "I can poke a hole clean through you with this."

Smoke spat blood on the ground. "We'll see."

Brandishing the razor-sharp steel, A.V. pounced. He

stabbed, jabbed, and cut with raw skill. His savage power and speed more than made up for his lack of refinement.

Smoke blocked and countered with every move he had. He parried the lighting-quick strikes with fists, forearms, and elbows.

A.V. countered his counter.

The knife snaked through Smoke's defenses.

Grinding his teeth, Smoke felt like a ball of fire exploded in his shoulder.

A.V. laughed.

CHAPTER 19

T HE HIGHER THEY SOARED, THE more Night Bird laughed. "I should drop you, but that's not the plan. I must say, that would be delightful. But Kane is obsessed with you, like some sort of prize." She sneered at Sid. "I don't see it."

Gathering her senses, Sid stared down at the ground. She felt as helpless as she was weightless. Night Bird's powerful wings beat against the wind, moving them away from the shipyard. "Where are you taking me?"

"You'll know when we get there."

Something flew up from the shipyard. It was Vormus. He wrapped his arms around Sid's body and tried to pull her free of Angi's talons.

"You!" Night Bird screamed. "Vormus, you are ever the pest!" She flapped harder. "Let go!"

"Oh, Angi, you are as lovely as ever, but I fear I cannot let go. This prize is mine."

Sid felt whatever power Vormus commanded pulling against her like a great weight.

Night Bird began to sink in the sky. Enraged, she

shrieked, "Release me, Vormus! Don't be a fool! Release me!"

"Release her, Angi, and I'll release you," Vormus said, and then he whispered in Sid's ear, "She's one of the more difficult women I know. We dated a century ago. She was quite entertaining but too needy for my liking in the end."

"Save the story and just get me back on earth," Sid choked out. Angi's talons were squeezing her to death. "Hurry."

The three of them spiraled in a downward pattern like a plane landing with one wing. Fifty feet. Thirty feet. Twenty feet. Night Bird squalled. The three of them hit hard.

Without hesitation, Vormus punched Night Bird in the face. Her grip loosened.

Sid squirmed free.

"Help Smoke," said Vormus. "He needs it. I'll handle her."

Sid took off at a full sprint. Dashing through the containers, she chased the sound of bodies slamming into metal. She darted back to the spot where the battle had started.

A.V. had Smoke hoisted over his head. He hurled Smoke into a wall of steel.

Smoke lay on the ground, unmoving.

Heart racing, Sid took a clip of bullets off her belt and flicked out the regular rounds with her thumb, one by one. *Please be in there!* The last bullet in the clip was green tipped. She didn't even know what it did. She snatched up her gun, dropped out the last magazine, stuffed in the new one, and charged the slide.

A.V. turned. "Huh?"

She squeezed the trigger. The bullet spun out of the chamber at hypersonic speed and smacked into A.V.'s chest.

A.V. the wolf man grunted. His part-wolf, part-man face looked down. The bullet had grafted itself to his skin like a tick. He plucked at it with his fingertips. "It tingles." His eyes slid Sid's way and froze. His jaw hung in an open expression. He looked like a wolf man who had just come from the taxidermist.

Groaning, Smoke knocked on A.V.'s leg. "He's stiff as a board."

Sid fanned her hand in front of A.V.'s eyes.

The eyes didn't move. A rugged sigh came from the shifter's mouth.

"It's probably going to wear off," she said. "We need to secure him."

A.V.'s hardened limbs didn't budge. Smoke put his flex cuffs away. "These are useless, but I have an idea." He picked A.V. up by the waist and walked him inside the shipping container. After unceremoniously dropping the wolf man on the floor, he stepped outside just as Vormus arrived.

The vampire shifter held Night Bird in his arms. She was unconscious. "She tires more easily than the rest." With a heave, he tossed her into the container like a hay bale.

Smoke closed the huge metal container and locked it

shut, checking that the locking mechanism was secure. "I think this was meant for us."

"Why's that?" Sid said, holding her ribs. It hurt to breathe.

Smoke lifted his hand and pointed. A painful grimace marked his face. A flatbed truck and loader were nearby.

Sid got it. Her attention zeroed in on Smoke's shoulder. His sweetheart suit was caked in blood. "John, you're hurt."

"Yeah, the werewolf stabbed me. Doesn't make much sense, does it?"

A hollow clapping sound came from nearby. Manson was sitting on a nearby container with his feet dangling over the edge. He was a blond-haired, blue-eyed boy again. "I found this mildly entertaining. You folks really make a great team."

"If you're so old, how'd you manage to climb up there?" Sid asked.

"Well, they have ladders."

"No they don't."

"Oh." Manson hopped off the container. He landed softly on his toes. "So maybe I'm a little spryer than I let on."

"You're a lot spryer than you let on." Sid picked up her guns and holstered them. "How come you didn't run?"

"Well, I never felt like a prisoner. And I could use the protection." He clasped his hands. "It looks like I'm in pretty good hands, even though Mister Smoke is bleeding. I have to say, that wound looks awfully painful. It's going to need more than just stitches. I'd say surgery.

Months of recovery. Oh, but you heal faster than most, don't you."

"Nothing extraordinary."

"I know better than that." Manson adjusted his navy-blue tie, then checked his sleeves. "I think this suit is done for. Can we swing by the mall? I need some new duds."

"Quiet." Smoke's eyes narrowed.

Sid caught the scuffle of soft shoes on the pavement. She braced herself against a nearby container, moving Manson back as she did so.

Who on earth do we have to deal with now?

CHAPTER 20

A PERSON PEEKED AROUND THE CORNER. Sid stuck her Glock in the man's temple. It was Mal Carlson.

"Easy now," the scientist said. His hands were up. "I'm here to help."

Sid disagreed. "You set us up."

"No, on the contrary, it wasn't me," said the disheveled man. "I didn't. Why would I set you up and then come here? I drove, for Pete's sake. Have you ever seen me drive before?"

"No, Asia always does."

Mal's shoulders drooped. "Uh-huh."

"Asia's a clone!" Sid said. Her stomach turned queasy. She shoved by Mal and upchucked right behind him. Leaning on the container, she tried to catch her breath. "Sorry about that. I guess all the excitement is getting to me."

Smoke laid his hand on her shoulder.

Sid waved him off. "Just give me some space. I need to breathe." She fanned her flushed face with her hands, taking in as deep a breath as she could. And wincing. It felt like someone had driven a nail into her ribs. "I think I've got a cracked rib. Damn."

"Just take it easy." Smoke took over. He gave Mal a little shove with his fingers. "What's going on?"

"I've been feeling a little worse each day for several weeks now. I wasn't sure what it was, but I never get sick. I dine on my fair share of crap, but I load up on vitamins and apricot seeds. After you left, I did a little more investigating on my own. Thanks to microtechnology, I was able to spy on my sweet Asia. The little witch from the Orient was poisoning me. Still, I lay low. That's when I caught your message. She sent you here, not me."

"Where's Asia now?" he asked.

"I have no idea. I pretended to be so sick I needed rest." He took off his glasses and huffed on them. "I still feel awful, but what she fed me is wearing off." He planted his glasses back on his nose. "I heard her leave not long after I pretended to sleep. If that was a clone, then where is my Asia, Smoke?" Mal sobbed. "Where?"

"We're working on that."

"You don't think she's dead, do you?"

Smoke looked down at Manson. The boy was chewing a piece of gum. He blew a bubble, shook his head. "No. She's probably at the power plant."

"The power plant?"

"Drake's power plant near Hillcrest Mausoleum." Manson popped his bubble. "They keep the cadavers in there."

"Who's this little creep?" Mal asked.

"Manson Bay, the keeper of secrets. He just let

another secret out." Smoke grabbed Manson by the tie. "Why didn't you mention that before?"

"Mysteries reveal themselves when the time is right. Now is the right time. Besides, you aren't going to be able to get in there without some sort of arsenal. I had hoped you would find the weapons cache you needed. You're screwed now."

Mal pulled his shoulders back. "The only one screwed is the one who stole my Asia." He looked Smoke in the eye. "I brought the weapons cache with me."

Sid hung back while the men checked out the midnight-blue Chevy Suburban Mal had driven to the shipyard. It was parked beside the Hellcat.

For some reason Manson stayed by Sid's side. He offered her a piece of gum. "You should try it. Bubble Yum watermelon. It's one of the few modern marvels I enjoy. Well, and *Seinfeld*. I think Shakespeare would have liked him."

"I'll pass," she said.

"Your breath is far from fabulous. I'd offer a mint if I had one."

She took the gum. Manson made a nice-looking young boy. He was sharp in his suit. But there were secrets behind his dark-blue eyes, and he carried himself like the ancient adult he was. "Why do you change from face to face?"

"It's just practice, really. I became a shifter when I was young. It was an accident. They hunted me. I learned to survive by changing my face, but I never identified with these monsters or anything. I didn't know what they were back then."

"It sounds like you've had a long and interesting life."

"Right on both counts." Manson cleared his throat. "But it nears its end. I've struggled for centuries knowing I wasn't on the right side of things, but I've been a coward. I let them control me. I created the clones for them. I regret it. They would have never known how to make them if I hadn't done it. I never thought they'd take it to the extreme they did."

Manson seemed innocent enough. She wanted to believe him. But she'd come up with her own rule of thumb. *All shifters are liars.* She played along.

Smoke hollered for her. "Sid, you have to see this."

The back of Mal's SUV was loaded with enough guns and ammo to start a small army. There were boxes of blue-, red-, and green-tipped rounds. Smoke was feeding rounds into an M-16 magazine. "This is going to get nasty."

"You need to take it easy. Your shoulder's still bleeding."

In a rough voice, Smoke replied, "I ain't got time to bleed."

"Well, you're going to make time to get stitched, Blain."

"I feel an action-packed marathon filled with tobacco and graphic violence coming on once this is over."

"Let's hope we can squeeze it in before the aliens, predators, and terminators arrive."

Everyone else had stopped what they were doing and was staring at them. Vormus said, "What's a terminator?"

"Five hundred pounds of steel under a hundred pounds of synthetic skin, steroids, and muscle." Smoke chuckled. "I'll be back."

"We could sure use Asia right now. I can't stitch a shoulder like she can."

"I'll do it," Manson volunteered. "You just have to trust me."

CHAPTER 21

THE FRONT PASSENGER SEAT WAS leaned all the way back in the Suburban. Smoke lay still in the leather chair. Manson sat in the rear seat overlooking Smoke's wound. He wore Smoke's goggles. The surgical tools in the boyish shifter's fingers moved with the precision and delicacy of a spider's spinnerets.

The large fighter was stripped down to the waist. His jaws clenched. "It feels like you're sticking a piece of rebar in there."

Sid stood just inside the open back door on the passenger side. Smoke's powerful grip held her hand tight. "You know you love the pain."

"Yeah, that burning, throbbing sensation really elates me."

"What," she smiled, "you aren't going to give me the 'Pain don't hurt' line?"

"I guess it slipped my mind."

"I'll be needing one of your little pills, Professor," Manson said to Mal, who was assisting from the driver's seat.

Startled, Mal said, "What do you mean?"

Manson rolled his eyes. "Not that kind. The supervitamins."

"Oh, I knew what you meant. Er, let me see. Uh, Sid, could you reach inside the glove box? There's a vial in there."

She retrieved the bottle of pills and twisted off the lid. "How's this going to help?" She started to put one in Smoke's open mouth.

"No, no, no," Manson said in an elderly voice. "Hand it to me."

She did.

The supervitamin was a large green gel pill with a glow to it. Manson held it between his forefinger and thumb. He eyeballed it, took a scalpel, and sliced it open. He squeezed out the contents into the wound.

"Woo!" Eyes wide, Smoke looked at Sid. "That's much better!"

"These vitamins have a powerful regenerating effect when applied directly to wounds." Manson leaned over the gap he had pulled open in Smoke's shoulder. "Heh, the muscle and tissue mends. You're fortunate the cut was so clean." He finished sewing up the wound. "Don't move it for a few hours. It should be much better by then, but there are no guarantees."

Smoke nodded.

"Now show me your cracked rib, and that hand," Manson said to Sid, reaching for the vial of pills.

"How'd you know the vitamins had that application?" Mal said. "Even I didn't know that."

"Because I created them, that's why."

The cabin quieted while Manson squirted the contents of two pills into a syringe and shot it into her rib and hand. At first it hurt like hell, but then it felt all better.

"Oh, I didn't create them for the likes of you. I created them for when the shifters make the initial transformation. It helps with the cloning process, too." Manson wiped down the tools and placed them back in the medical kit. "They typically have a disastrous effect on humans. I marvel that you can use them, but it must be the shifter blood in you."

Sid got that sinking feeling again. She spoke up. "I've been curious where all this equipment comes from. If the FBI isn't supplying it, then who is?"

Mal held up a finger. "I've been under the impression it was the people who ran the Black Slate. They're the ones who contacted me. It was easy enough to believe it was from a covert military operation."

Manson chuckled like an old man who was the only one with the answer to the puzzle. "I hate to use the word 'gullible,' because it's not entirely true. Yes, a government entity is behind these gifts you receive. But those factions are run by powers and principalities that are difficult to understand. There's good within their ranks, but there's a dark force, too. The Drake runs the evil faction. They use the clones to infiltrate the government ranks. They're trying to out the Church of Nigil."

Sid leaned forward. "The Church of Nigil?"

"The shifters have been around since ancient times. I'm certain you've figured out that much." Manson scooted down his seat and pushed down his armrest.

He turned the cabin light off. "They've been a threat on and off throughout all history. In the Dark Ages, the shifters—typically a bunch of crude and savage individuals who worked alone—began working with one another. That's when some of the earliest knights were formed by a warrior named Nigil. He was a devout man, a minister of the faith. He worked quietly and diligently behind the scenes. To this day, there are many unknown followers of the Church of Nigil. They keep the forces of evil at bay. However, with the help of the clones, the Drake, the shifters, and the likes of Kane are having these good members of the old guard eliminated. It's a very quiet but devastating extraction." He hitched his thumb over his shoulder. "They're the ones behind the Black Slate, the Church of Nigil, but now the Drake has them on the run. It's a nasty business."

"I've never heard of this church," Mal said.

"They are careful to wipe out all traces of their existence, but they walk like angels among us—not so much for my benefit but for yours."

"You say they're knights. Do they fight?" Smoke asked.

"They fight with thought, not fists."

Sid soaked in her thoughts. The answer to every mystery was another mystery. She leaned back and gazed at the stars in the sky. *I guess I'll never have the answers to everything. Not in this lifetime I won't. I'll just march forward on faith.*

Smoke took her by the hand and pulled her into the car. "It's time to take out the clones."

CHAPTER 22

THEY'LL BE EXPECTING A.V. AND Angi back at the Drake compound." Vormus stood beside the containers with a bored look on his face. "I suggest you execute your plan soon."

Sid, Smoke, and Mal were standing around the hood of Mal's SUV, going over the plan with Manson. The boy shifter had drawn them a map, and he said he had told them everything he could think of about the compound.

Drake Headquarters was nestled in the woods. The concrete building was built like a bunker. The windows were small on the three levels of flooring. The security was tight. There was a checkpoint for all traffic going in and coming out. A barbed-wire fence secured at least a mile-wide perimeter.

"You have the pea coats, deaders, and shifters," Manson said, rubbing his nose. "They don't take any chances with the Pyramid. With me gone, they're going to be a little more paranoid from now on."

"What about electronic security? Cameras, pass

codes, key fobs, magnetic locks?" Sid asked as she pressed new bullets into her clips.

"Huh, well, needless to say, the Drake uses plenty of technology, but they're pretty old fashioned about this place. They don't want a digital record on their dealings. Needless to say, they don't want any strangers prowling about. If someone strange shows up, they kill them. Or clone them. They don't want to be hacked, either. Sure, they entertain the elites with recordings of their fights and battles, but that doesn't happen at this location. It's top secret."

"But they have to run power to the pyramid server, don't they?" Smoke asked. Automatic pistols hung on his hips. Machine guns were strapped to his back. He taped two weapons' magazines together with duct tape.

"The server does have power. It's enough power to run a small city. It's in the basement, deep, where it's cool. It's in a glass vault. Shatterproof stuff. I'm not even sure if a bomb could take it out." Manson shrugged. "Destroying it won't be easy. Just getting down there will be a feat in itself."

Smoke said to Sid, "Sounds like a job for James Bond."

"James who?" Vormus asked.

"It sure doesn't sound like we can go blasting through there," she said. Based off what Manson had told her, she didn't like the odds. But she felt compelled to do it. She needed to find her sister and niece. She couldn't help but think something bad was about to happen. "How confident are you that Kane now resides at this compound?"

"Oh, he's there. He doesn't have anywhere else to be at the moment."

"How can you be so sure?"

Manson shrugged. "I suppose I could be wrong, but are we going after Kane or the server? We have to take down one thing at a time."

"I concur with Manson," Vormus said. "I believe Kane is there hiding like the rat he is. He knows you have to come after him if he doesn't haul you in there himself. He just wants the advantage. The shifters who serve him want to redeem themselves. Now's the time to take him."

Typing on his laptop, Mal said, "Let's not forget we need to find my Asia. She's in there too, and we don't need any collateral damage. I won't have any part of that. I have an idea though."

"What is it?"

"Servers need to stay cool. If we cut the power to its ventilation systems, won't the server shut down?"

Manson blew a gum bubble until it popped. "Perhaps. It runs hot, but there will be back-up generators. Those will need to go down too. Everything tied to the server will have plenty of security. I didn't have a hand in those systems. I just handle the clone programming. Also, just because the server is shut down doesn't mean the cadavers will waken."

"You speak like they are dead," Mal said, his voice torn with emotion.

"Well, they're in a suspended state. It's more like a coma one never wakes up from. Many die during the process."

"John, can I have a word with you?" Sid asked.

Her husband moved out of everyone else's earshot with her.

"I'm not very comfortable with this, and I don't trust either of them. It sounds like we're about to walk into a bigger net."

"I guess we won't know for sure until we get there, but I'd rather roll in than wait and see. Let me try to steer this thing, and we'll see if they try to dissuade us."

"You just want to play with those weapons."

"I want to waste shifters." He slapped a magazine into his rifle and slung the weapon over his back. "I'm not buying that they can't be killed. Everything can be killed. We just need to find a quicker way to do that. We'll figure it out."

Sid put her hands on his face, went up on tiptoes, and kissed him. "Okay, I'll follow your lead. If I can't trust you, I can't trust anybody. How's the shoulder?"

"Good enough to support my trigger finger." He kissed her back. "How's the rib and hand?"

"Good enough to do this." She kissed him soundly, putting her body into it.

When they'd made their way back to the others, Smoke laid out his plan. "Operation Trojan Horse."

"Sounds original," Vormus said.

Smoke pointed to the truck and the container with the prisoners in it. "They're expecting the truck, so we'll send them the truck. All we have to do is convince Wolf Man and Night Bird to drive."

"That'll never happen," Vormus said. "They won't

willingly betray Kane. He has them wrapped around his finger."

"I can help with that." Manson's small body grew. The seams of his suit burst.

Everyone took a step back.

Transforming before their eyes, Manson became the spitting image of A.V. He said, "I'm going to need some bigger clothes."

Smoke slapped him on the shoulder. "And I'm going to need to know exactly where those generators are."

CHAPTER 23

S ID RODE IN THE CAB of the container truck. Manson, now disguised as A.V., drove. He struggled with shifting gears. He worked the long shift with his hairy, clawed fingers like an amateur. He'd stalled at two stoplights already. Sid's nerves were wearing thin.

"Why don't you let me drive?" she said. "You're doing horrible."

"No, I always liked driving. I used to do a lot more of it in the good old days. Those Model Ts were slow but fun. I could get away with it back then when I was a kid. No one cared how old you were. Lots of kids drove back then, those whose parents could afford to let them drive their expensive machines. Now I look too young, and you have to have a license to do just about everything but pee." The light turned green. He popped the clutch and pushed the accelerator, and the big truck rumbled forward. Bouncing in his seat, he said, "See, I'm getting better."

"It looks to me like you can take on whatever form

you want. You don't have to stay a kid. So what are you, a doppelganger like Reginald?"

"Eh, sort of. Old Reggie is a clever bird. Very powerful. Almost as powerful as Kane himself. I'm all boy in the day, but I can change form once night falls. But let's keep that between us. The others don't know I can do it. Hee hee! I'm a kid. I'm supposed to be sneaky."

"Why only at night?"

"Evil thrives in the darkness, I suppose. It's a mystic thing. Just imagine where we would be without the light. Did you know more than eighty percent of all crimes are committed at night?"

"Yeah, I read that once."

Manson looked right at her. "Really?"

"No. Stop looking at me. Just keep your eyes on the road."

"You don't like this face, do you."

"I hate that face." Sid pushed back into her seat and set her stare on the road.

"The first experience with a shifter leaves a deep impression. It taints you. No experience with the supernatural is unforgettable. In your case, I'd say temptation overcame you." The truck banged over some potholes. "The seductive nature. The raw power. It sucks you in. There is a promise of great pleasure. Very few can resist it."

Sid's throat tightened. She remembered the encounter with A.V. like it was yesterday. The temptation was etched in her mind forever. A craving had overcome her. She'd wanted to succumb. Embrace it. Smoke's words had brought her to her senses. *Pancakes and butterflies.* She smiled.

"What?" Manson asked.

"Nothing. Question. I shot A.V. with silver bullets. He clearly feared them. How come it didn't kill him?"

"Oh, that's all stuff from your picture shows. Sure, silver is the weakness in his case. Every shifter has one. But once they removed the bullet, he was revived. Heh, we are truly hard to kill."

"So does Vormus have a weakness for wooden stakes and crucifixes?"

Manson lifted his shoulders. "Maybe. It's different for everyone. I don't think they even know their own weakness. That's why they're so cocky. But it trips them up sometimes. One shifter had a severe allergy to pewter. She was killed by a fork and a butter knife. Heh. That was in the eighteenth century. They wore really big hats back then."

"I'm surprised you're willing to ride right into the lion's den, Manson."

"You aren't surprised. You're suspicious, and I don't fault you. Well, I'm taking a new side." His voice became cryptic. "The signs abound. The sky falls. The walls close in. The end is near."

Goose bumps rose on her arms even with the second skin on. She sat in the quiet for the rest of the ride, going through the game plan.

Now's not the time to worry about what he is or isn't going to do. Just focus on what you need to do, Sid.

Manson drove the truck onto a private road that split from the highway. A green sign read Hillcrest Road. Also, a Drake Properties sign was posted at the split, along with several notable "No Trespassing" and "Private

Property" signs. The winding road snaked up into the hills for miles. Trees of all sorts lined both sides. Leaves bent on the branches as the truck rolled by. The road flattened out at the top. They passed a mausoleum on the right. The building was surrounded by hundreds of grave markers in an overgrown field. The mausoleum itself looked to be big enough to hold at least a dozen bodies inside the belly of its sandstone framework. A monolith of stone sat facing the moonlight. Two urns sat on the ledges that confined the steps leading up to the iron door of the mausoleum. Four thick stone pillars held up the front of the roof.

At least I don't see any gargoyles.

Ahead were the guard shack and the perimeter fence. The fencing was ten feet high. The top was covered in coils of barbed wire. Behind it was a stone building three stories tall with small windows, just as Manson had described. There were parking places outside, and a ramp led below the building. Dim lights illuminated some of the windows.

Two men in pea coats stepped out of the guard shack and greeted them with M-16s.

Manson brought the truck to a stop. "I'll do the talking."

The guards flanked the passenger and driver's-side doors. A third man stepped out from behind the shack. A giant of a man over eight feet tall. His hair stood up on top of his head in patches. He wore a beige, Carhartt-like work suit.

Lance!

CHAPTER 24

T HE HUGE TEENAGER STOOD BETWEEN the truck and the gate. He stooped, staring right at the windshield, small eyes squinting.

Manson rolled down his window.

The guard climbed up on the semi-truck's doorstep. His eyes popped open when he met Manson's in A.V. form.

"Special delivery," Manson said. "And don't ever get in my face again."

The flat-nosed guard held his ground. "Who's the girl? I don't recognize her."

"She's the delivery, fool!" Manson shoved the man off the side of his truck. The guard fell on the ground, popped up, and with a nasty glance over his shoulder at Manson, he headed over to Lance.

Manson said to Sid, "You seem to recognize that big fella. Got a name?"

"Lance. We crossed with him a little ways back at Titus Tolliver's mortuary. I'm a bit surprised he's here. He's a loner."

"A shifter that big has nowhere else to go. Hmm, I wonder if he knows A.V."

Lance approached.

"I guess we're about to find out." Sid put on a long face. Lance's big head almost filled the window. His little eyes got big. "You! Why isn't she secured?"

"She's not going anywhere, Lance. Her loved one is hostage in the back."

"They should both be in there," Lance said. "Kane's not going to like this. Where's the bird lady?"

Manson leaned toward the windshield and glanced up in the sky. "I'm sure she'll be landing any moment now, if she hasn't already. Why, do you still have a thing for her?"

Lance gaped. "What thing?"

"Oh, people talk. They say you give the little lady a lot of leers. I can't blame you. She's a fine wine even to the likes of myself, though a little moody."

"I don't remember you being so talky," Lance said. He stuck his entire head through the window. Sid crammed into the back of her seat. Lance sniffed. "Anyone back in there?"

"The truck cab? Uh, no, you can see for yourself." Manson popped his door open.

"Forget it." Lance looked at Sid. "You burnt my hair."

"I don't care."

"You will." Lance walked away. He snatched a radio from one of the guards. The radio looked like a credit card in his big hand. He said something. A few seconds later, he gave a nod and then dropped the radio on the ground. Using his hand like a grizzly bear's paw, he grabbed the heavy gate by the chain-link fencing and walked it open, waving the truck through.

Manson jammed the truck into gear, hit the gas, and stalled.

"Really?"

He started the engine again. "Sorry, but this clutch is jumpy."

"No, your driving is shitty."

"What do you expect? It's been decades." He hit the gas, the truck jumped forward, and he eased it through the gate. Lance stepped in front of the truck. Arms swinging easily and with giant strides, the colossal teen led them inside the compound. "Looks like things are going to be chippy. I hope things work out. I don't recall seeing this many people about."

Sid counted men in pea coats. They stood inside the windows and were scattered in the parking lot. Each one carried an Uzi. She noted a head and a rifle barrel on top of the building. Men marched along the fence. There were man-like figures, too. Deaders. They wore clothing like men but walked like zombies. Their jaws were slack and eyes sunken as they creeped around the plaza. "And you made those things?"

"I'm not fully responsible for the juices that keep them alive. Much was passed down through the ages. At least you know stopping their hearts stops them."

"Unless they have body armor on. Which, by the looks of them, they do. Morning glory. How did I ever get into this?"

"The same way we all do. Destiny."

"I don't know about that."

A twelve-foot-high garage door rolled open, just like the ones they used in the federal buildings. Lance crossed the barrier and walked down the ramp into a huge garage bay lit up by fluorescent lights. Lance waved them over toward the middle and motioned for them to stop. Aside from the way they had come in, the only other ways out were a stairwell door and an elevator. The roll-up garage door closed behind them, sealing them inside.

"If you haven't prayed yet, now might be the time to do so. I respect that. We'll be having company soon."

Sid mentally said a prayer. She'd done it several times since they left.

Jesus, I know you know what you're doing, but I'm not sure what I'm doing. Give me strength.

The stairwell door burst open. A dozen pea coats came out. Rushing over on booted feet, they surrounded the truck. The elevator doors split open. She expected to see the brawny Kane. She got a bigger surprise. It was her.

Manson leaned forward. "Oh my, that's you. How quaint."

Samone, Sid's shifter clone, was dressed in a sweetheart suit the same as Sid's. She was identical in every aspect—aside from the cruel sneer on her lips. She wasn't alone. Titus Tolliver was in full gargoyle form on one side. Swift Venison, the were-rat in slacks, was on the other. She hoped to see her sister, but there wasn't a sign of Allison anywhere. "Are you sure Kane is here?"

"I'm not entirely positive, but where else would he be? He's cautious. Can you blame him? Why else send in a clone?"

"To rattle me and Smoke."

"That's what I'd do." Manson shut off the engine, opened his door, and made his way out of the cab. Sid did too. "Package delivered," Manson said.

"I can see that," Samone said. Her eyes never left Sid's face. "At least half of it. Am I to assume the other half of this dynamic duo is inside the container?"

"Even Houdini couldn't make it out of this container. Plus, he's bound up. All secure."

Arms crossed over her chest, Samone stood eye to eye with Sid. "We'll see. Rexor! Thorgrim! Come!"

Two huge men stepped out from behind the support columns of the garage and shambled over. They were the same pair of giants that had tangled with Smoke before, bigger and brawnier than Lance. Both wore heavy burnt-orange jumpsuits. Shaggy, long hair hung over their shoulders. Rexor was bearded, Thorgrim clean shaven.

Glancing at the container, Samone said, "Bring it down."

In a feat of awesome power, the giants snapped the chains that held the container secure on the truck bed. Using their fingertips, they picked it up. Together, they walked it off the flatbed, shaking the metal box and laughing. "Heh-heh-heh-heh!"

"It's not a present. Just set it down," Samone said.

Thorgrim dropped his end.

Boom!

"I said set it down, not drop it!"

Rexor eased down his end.

Sid's mind scrambled for another plan. She hadn't expected to see so many powerful enemies in one place.

She fully hadn't expected to see the giants. *Screw this, I'm not taking any chances.* She bit open the supervitamin stuck in her cheek and swallowed.

"Go ahead, Thorgrim. Open it up and see what's inside."

The giant handled the metal locking bars with ease. Metal scraped over the mechanism with an annoying squeak that echoed inside the garage. Many hardened faces cringed.

Looking at Samone with big, sad eyes, Thorgrim said in a cavernous voice, "Sorry." He opened the doors, stooped, and peered inside, then hunkered down and crammed inside. "Hello?" His voice echoed in the chamber. He shuffled back out. "It's empty."

Samone locked her fingers on Sid's arm. "Where is he?"

CHAPTER 25

I N THE AIR, VORMUS FOLLOWED the truck from the shipyard to the Drake Compound. He waited just below the tree line when the truck came to a stop at the gate. Once the truck was through and inside the building, he made his move. Floating above the treetops, he rose higher in a huge arc and then hung suspended above the roof. He counted four men roosted on top of the building, leaning over the north, south, east, and west ledges. Each was armed with a machine gun. In the center of the roof was the chiller plant. The fans from the three refrigeration units spun at high speeds, sending gusts of wind into the air.

I can't believe I'm doing this.

He held a pack of C4 plastic explosives in his hand. Staring at it, he shook his head.

So not me.

Vormus's part was to take down the heating and cooling system in hopes of damaging the server. There weren't any guarantees it would work, but it was only part of the plan. This was also a distraction. It was Smoke's plan. Vormus didn't like it, but he complied.

He drifted down like a falling feather onto the roof and nestled himself between the units, where he then stuck three packs of C4 to three different units and filled the malleable plastic with the remote detonator pins.

"Don't move," a guard said. The man had crept up into his blind spot. The barrel of his gun was pointed at Vormus's face.

Slowly, Vormus turned. "That's no way to treat the air conditioner repairman."

"You don't look like a repairman to—"

Vormus ripped the rifle out of the guard's hands. He punched the man in the face, crushing his nose. The powerful blow sent the man backward, where he tripped and skipped on the roof with a loud scuffle.

"Hey, what's going on over there?" another guard cried out.

Back pressed against the chiller, Vormus sensed the men closing in.

So much for discretion.

Vormus burst into action. Toes lifting off the roof, he glided into the blind spot of the first guard he saw. He put the man in a headlock and squeezed. The guard's neck popped. He let the body down and moved on. He found the third guard leaning over the first guard he had punched. He swooped in and punched the man in the temple.

The fourth guard appeared around the corner of the chiller unit. "Move a muscle and I'll send a hundred bullets through you."

Vormus lifted his palms and searched out the man's eyes.

The guard looked right into Vormus's hypnotizing eyes. The man's body locked up.

Holding the man's gaze, the vampire floated over to him and pulled the rifle from his hands. "Normally, I'd twist your head from your shoulders, little man. Fortunately for you, I'm beginning to enjoy this covert thing. It's not as sticky."

The rigid guard stood with a spacy look in his eyes.

Vormus armed a chunk of C4 and stuck it in the man's pea coat pocket. "I really do hate pea coats. If I could destroy them all, I think I would."

"Not everyone shares your sense of style," said a familiar voice.

"Huh?" Vormus turned. He couldn't hide his surprise. "Reginald. And what brings the doppelganger out on this fair night?"

Wearing a suit, the slender salt-and-pepper-haired man looked like he'd just left a business meeting. He sucked on a cigarette. The tobacco burned bright orange. Smoke vapors drifted in the air. A silent drone hovered in the air about twenty feet above their heads. "We've been watching you since the moment you dropped in." He opened up his hand. "Hand over the detonator."

"And fail my task in this secret mission? Oh, I couldn't do that. I'm hoping to get a medal for it."

Reginald slipped off his coat. "I tell you what. Let's make it fun." He blew smoke out of his nostrils and set the cigarette aside with the fire still burning. "Kane and I discussed your betrayal, and he has a deal for you. A simple one. You won't have to make all this racket and create a big mess. Beat me, and you can go in peace." He was rolling up his sleeves. "It's a good deal. Besides, your new little allies, Sid and Smoke, were doomed the moment they entered the building."

CHAPTER 26

T HE GRIP OF SAMONE'S HAND had the power of a vise. Sid tried to pull away, but Samone held tight. "Where is he?"

"I don't know," Sid said. "He was in there when we left. Maybe the stupid giant isn't looking hard enough."

"Shut up!"

"He's slipped us," suggested Manson, still posing as A.V.

Samone's brows lifted. "Oh, so you think he *slipped* us? Are you stupid enough to think anything slipped by us?" Samone laughed. "We knew you were coming since the moment you left, Manson."

Manson's eyes enlarged. "I beg your pardon."

Titus Tolliver, the gargoyle, walked up behind Manson and locked his stony fingers around his wrists. "Nice try, fool."

"I beg your pardon, Samone, but you're making a big mistake. I'm A.V."

Samone just rolled her eyes at that. "So where are the real A.V. and Night Bird?"

"I have no idea."

"It doesn't matter. At least half the problem is solved." Samone jerked Sid's arm. "Let's take you to Kane."

"Rough hand me again, clone, and I'll bust you in the face," Sid said.

"Is that so?" Samone tugged again. "I'd like to see you try it, mortal."

"You will soon enough, you soulless bitch."

Samone smacked Sid hard in the face.

With all eyes on the twin women, a new voice interrupted the scene. In an oddly familiar yodel, a man said, "Helloooooooooo."

Shoulders swiveled. Heads turned. Heels pivoted.

Smoke stood on top of the container, armed to the teeth. Two L.A.W. rockets rested on his broad shoulders.

Samone tossed her head back and laughed. Gloating, she said, "Smoke, surely you don't think you can escape this complex?"

"That depends on how reasonable we're all willing to be. All I want is the girl," Smoke said, aiming the rockets at Samone.

"And if we refuse?"

"Then your fuhrer has no prize."

"What?' Samone said.

Several faces had puzzled looks. Thorgrim and Rexor scratched their heads.

Swift Venison, the rat man, stroked the rat tail that hung over his shoulder and chimed in. "I believe he just quoted from *Raiders of the Lost Ark*. Actually, I believe you both did."

Samone sneered at the rat man.

"Though it was unintentional," the rat man finished. He cackled. "Humorous though. Even I admit to enjoying how this mortal banters in the direst situations."

"Why don't you come down from your perch, Smoke? Just think how much you can enjoy yourself with the both of us, hm, dearie?" She hugged Sid. "Haven't you ever had twins before? Double your pleasure? Double your fun?"

"Double your enjoyment?" the rat man added.

"Will you shut up?" Samone said. "Come on now, Smokie. Let's talk about this."

The giants spread out, flanking Smoke's position.

"Take another step, and you're going to find out what rockets do in a confined space like this," Smoke warned.

Thorgrim and Rexor froze. Their heavy eyes drifted back to Samone.

"What will you do, Smokie, drop the entire building on us? Now that would be foolish. We wouldn't die, but you most certainly would."

"You know, I'm not really buying into this shifter immortality thing. I'm pretty confident you won't survive instant disintegration." He panned the L.A.W. rocket tubes toward the giants. "I'm quite willing to unleash a test fire. Do you behemoths want to volunteer?"

"That mortal is crazy," Samone said to Sid. "He's going to get you killed."

"True. He loves me to death." Sid felt the vitamin start to kick in. *Yes!* "Too bad you'll never know love, Samone. Oh, what a feeling." In a super-fast move, she reversed Samone's arm behind her back. The clone had strength beyond her appearance, but now so did Sid. She cranked up the pressure so hard the woman's shoulder popped out of the socket.

"Argh!" Samone moaned. "Screw the rockets! Take them down! Take them down now!"

The giants moved in.

Smoke depressed the rubber triggers on the rockets.

Sid shoved Samone aside, covered her ears, squeezed her eyes shut, and hunkered down.

CHAPTER 27

"I sn't this a bit old fashioned, even for you?" Vormus said to Reginald.

The shifters squared off.

Reginald shrugged. "Even I need a challenge from time to time. It makes me feel alive. Isn't that what you want, Vormus, to feel alive again? Now is your chance. You can be free to pursue your life as you want it."

Vormus held the detonator in his hand. His thumb toyed with the trigger. There was enough C4 to blow the entire roof off the building. It would end him, too.

"Go ahead, Vormus. Squeeze the trigger. You stand about the same chance of surviving as you do in a fight with me."

"If it's such a mismatch, why bother to fight at all?"

"True," Reginald replied. "But who knows, maybe you'll get a lucky punch in."

"Reginald, you aren't half as durable as you think." He set down the trigger. "And I'm twice as strong as you realize."

"We'll see about that." The doppelganger spread his

arms wide and wiggled his hands. "Let the games begin." Reginald charged.

Vormus caught the man's bull rush in his chest. He tried to lock up the man's arms.

Reginald's fists smacked hard into Vormus's face with the jarring force of hammers. He overwhelmed Vormus with fists that swarmed him like bees. The superior fighter peppered him with blow after blow.

Vormus's body absorbed punishment that would have broken an ordinary man. He dropped to a knee.

Reginald kicked him in the chest. The blow sent him flying into the chiller.

Vormus shook it off. Something felt funny. He touched his nose, and it was out of place on his face. Shoving his nose back into its original position with a crunch, he said, "You'd think the nose would be tougher." He pushed his way back up to his feet. "You've always been overaggressive. You can pummel me all night, but you still won't break me."

"This is just a warm-up for when the real battle begins. Believe me, it's coming. But you won't be here to see it. Kane wants you dead once and for all." Reginald picked up his cigarette and took a puff. Blowing the smoke through his teeth, he said, "Let's keep dancing." With the cigarette pinched between his fingers, he said, "Oh wait. A moment please." Reginald reached behind the chiller.

What is he up to now?

The doppelganger withdrew a pair of Arabian swords. The majestically crafted steel blades' curved edges caught the bright glow of the moonlight, giving them a lifelike quality of their own. Reginald tossed one of the blades.

Vormus snatched it out of the air.

"As I understand it, you're a much better swordsman than you are a fighter." Reginald cut his blade through the air a few more times. "At least you had better hope so."

Thumbing the keen edge of the Arabian steel, Vormus said, "Your mistake. I'm much better with steel than you are as a fighter. Big mistake, Reginald. An utter catastrophe." The blade took off a sliver of his skin when he tested it. The steel wasn't anything ordinary. No, it was the same metal as the knives Smoke and Sid used. It could cut just about anything, even a shifter's skin.

"They say a shifter is only as formidable as his parts, useless as an infant when those parts are missing." Reginald bent his knees into a stance. "Eventually, one of us is going to lose his head over this."

Vormus approached with confidence. "The headless shifter won't be me." He struck.

The well-honed blades clashed together. Using his size and length, Vormus pushed the smaller shifter backward. Steel battered steel.

Reginald laughed. "You're a horrible swordsman. I can't believe it. I knew you wouldn't be as good as me, but with all your divine skills, I never imagined you'd be this bad." He put Vormus on the defensive with a display of lightning-quick chops and cuts. The Arabian sword slit the side of the vampire's ribs. Reginald jumped back, pumping a fist and screaming, "Score!"

"No need to gloat. The fight isn't over yet," Vormus remarked.

But it was over. Reginald was twice the fighter he was. Vormus had been feasting on the weak for years, but Reginald had been the shifter who hunted down any threats to the Drake, including overzealous heroes like Sid and Smoke.

"I must say I'm disappointed. After all, you did give your brother quite the tussle back at the mansion. You actually shook him up. It makes me wonder."

"Perhaps you should lead the shifters," Vormus suggested.

"No, too much responsibility. I'm perfectly satisfied being the best at one thing."

"It's good to know your limits." Vormus eased forward with his free hand behind his back. "Shall we carry on?"

"Eager for your own funeral, I see. Who knows, you might even wind up in the mausoleum. After all, you are Kane's family."

"Do tell." Vormus snaked in and stabbed at Reginald's chest.

The doppelganger swatted the blade aside. With a twist of his wrist, he disarmed Vormus. He held the steel tip on Vormus's neck.

Vormus felt the edge nicking his skin. "You're quick. Well done."

"I'm the best."

"It's a shame I'll never get to see your trophy room."

"No, but I might just have your head mounted on the wall."

Vormus swallowed. He'd never been so close to death

since the days before he became a shifter. Now, at the foothold of death, he realized he'd never see the light again. "I don't suppose you're open for negotiation."

"No, not with so many eyes watching, but I'm sure the elite have enjoyed this. Goodbye, Vormus." Reginald cocked back to deliver the final swing.

But just then, the entire building shook with the sound of a muffled thunderclap from way down below.

The doppelganger teetered.

Vormus shoved the man away. Moving with the speed of a frightened rabbit, he snatched up the detonator that lay nearby and leapt into the air. His body lifted from the rooftop at startling speed.

Reginald looked up at him, gaping, and yelled, "Coward!"

A drone whizzed in front of Vormus's face. He noted the tiny camera lens staring at him like an eye. He held up the detonator. "Enjoy the show, assholes." He squeezed the trigger.

The chillers erupted in a series of blinding explosions. Wrecked steel and hunks of building showered the air. The rooftop became a smoking and burning crater.

Reginald was nowhere to be found.

Vormus snatched up the drone and looked into its lens. "See you soon, dear brother." He ripped off the propellers and dropped the drone into the fire.

CHAPTER 28

GUNFIRE ERUPTED AROUND SMOKE JUST as he squeezed the triggers. The first rocket smote the giant Thorgrim in the chest with a mighty *kaboom*! The second rocket did the same to Rexor. The explosive's sound was deafening, its concussive force bone jarring. His entire body juddered from the impact. His ears rang like bells. Half the lights in the garage were out. The pea coat guards were on hands and knees. Several held their ears. Others were out cold. Smoke waded through the haze toward Sid. He found her balled up on the ground.

Her dark eyes were alert and searching. She found his face. "You're crazy!"

"I thought that was what we planned on."

Fingers tapping her ears, she said, "What?" She started gearing up with whatever Smoke had hanging off him. She snapped a belt of ammo around her waist.

"What?" he said back.

She shook her head and took a strap from his shoulder. "Where's Samone?"

He caught a glimpse of the clone scuttling into the

fire exit. She was accompanied by the shifters Venison and Titus.

Gunfire cracked off.

Smoke dropped to a knee.

The pea coat forces had gathered. A hail of semi-automatic gunfire spewed out of their muzzles.

"Let's waste them."

Smoke and Sid picked the men off one by one. The blue-tipped bullets ripped through the armor the pea coat guards wore underneath. They went down in cries and groans. Most of them went dead silent.

Squeezing off round after round, Smoke didn't care. It was war.

It's us or them.

Sid marched right into the line of enemy fire like a gallant archangel. Every shot she fired hit the mark.

Lance stepped out from behind one of the circular support columns.

She unloaded a clip in his chest with a rapid *budda-budda-budda* sound.

Lance dusted off his chest. "Your bullets might sting, but they won't kill me. This suit is bulletproof."

Sid popped out the magazine and loaded the second clip taped to the first, quick as she could whistle. Without looking back at him, she said, "Smoke, no more center mass. It's going to have to be head shots from now on. I like head shots."

Lance stepped forward. "Just try me."

Sid took aim. "One more step and I'm going to turn your brains into dog chow." She charged the machinegun handle. "Try me. These rounds are explosive."

Focused on Sid, out of the corner of Smoke's eyes, he saw Rexor and Thorgrim start to rise. "Sid, the tide's rising." He switched to the explosive rounds. "How many bullets is it going to take to put these suckers down?"

With her senses, strength, and agility enhanced, Sid was ready for anything.

Lance stared right at her, wary.

She didn't know whether she could stop the giant or not. She felt the presence of the bigger, more powerful giant fill the room.

Lance bent at the knees. His oversized body leaned forward.

Aw, Screw this!

"Goodbye, Lance." She squeezed the trigger, and a hail of bullets burst into Lance's face like angry hornets. One small explosion after the other rocked the garage.

Lance stumbled backward. His arms slapped at the air. Chunks of his head flew off. He screamed, "Noooooo!" He bounced off the column then fell hard on his back, crushing a crawling deader beneath him. He looked up at Sid with half his face missing. Somehow, he spoke.

"Why?"

Sid emptied the clip on the abomination. "I hope this keeps a bad man down."

"Sid!" Smoke cried out. He was firing round after round at the giants' heads, but they were covering their faces with their forearms. His clip emptied. He started to reload.

The bearded giant snatched up a dead pea coat's body and hurled it at Smoke.

Unable to avoid the colossal missile, he was sent sprawling.

Both giants pounced.

Sid loaded another clip of blue tips and fired them into the giant Thorgrim's ear.

"Eeeyargh!" the giant screamed. He swatted at Sid.

She slipped from his clutches while peppering his face with bullets.

He covered up again.

She fired shot after shot, keeping the giant at bay. "Smoke, we have a big problem. We're going to need bigger bullets to stop these things."

Slipping in and out of the giant's grasp, he said, "Try negotiating."

"I don't think they know what that means."

Every time the giant peeked through its forearms, Sid fired through them at him.

It drew forth grunt after grunt, but the giant lumbered forward until he closed into point-blank range.

Sid fired everything she had, marveling at how the sleeves of the suit the giant wore held up against bullets that ripped through stone and steel. "Damn chemical engineers. They can think up anything."

Thorgrim backed her into the corner and peeked through his forearms. "Boo!"

Sid pulled the special knife from her utility belt. "Boohoo!" She jammed it into the giant's foot. It sank through meat and bone.

Thorgrim chuckled. The monstrous, hairy man's limbs closed around her body.

She dove between his legs.

The giant turned and fell. His foot was pinned to the cement floor by the knife. He ripped it out with a grunt, rose back onto his feet, and chased after Sid, hurdling the dead bodies.

"Any ideas, John?"

Rexor had Smoke in a bear hug. Her husband's face was red as a beet. He kept cracking the giant right between the eyes with the butt of his assault rifle and screaming, "Detonator! Detonator! It's inside the container. Hurry!"

She rushed into the huge steel box. There was a concealed panel compartment at the front where Smoke had hidden while they drove in. It was something they'd set up before they left. Inside was the entire weapons cache. Sid opened up an ammo box filled with C4. The detonation plugs were set. She grabbed the detonator and two blocks of C4 and raced outside.

Smoke was hitting the giant in the face like he was trying to crack open a fortune cookie as he screamed, "What is the riddle steel? What is the riddle steel?"

"Smoke!" Sid yelled.

His head rolled her way. Eyes wide, he dropped the weapon.

Sid tossed him one pack of C4.

Without looking, he snatched it from the air and shoved it in the nine-footer's mouth. He pinched Rexor's nose with one hand and held his lower jaw shut with the other, saying, "Steel isn't strong. Flesh is stronger."

Rexor swallowed. "Gulp!"

Smoke looked at Sid and said in words he could hardly hear, "Detonate this infidel defiler!"

CHAPTER 29

"ANYTHING TO GET YOU TO stop quoting lines from *Conan the Barbarian*." Sidney pressed the trigger on the detonator.

The insides of Rexor's body made a *poomf* sound. The giant's belly bulged, expanded within the seams of his jumpsuit, and collapsed.

Smoke slipped free of the monster man's clutches and landed on his knees, huffing for breath.

Rexor's eyes—which seemed to be the size of headlights—glazed over. His head and shoulders sank into his suit. A strange type of blood and guts seeped out of his pant legs.

Sid had a sickening feeling the innards of the tremendous man had been obliterated. She couldn't contain her gawking as the top of Rexor's body collapsed one way and his legs went the other. The huge man groaned. His fingers clutched at the air as he fell and made a gross-sounding *splat*.

Thorgrim rushed over to his brother's side and scooped his mangled body up into his arms. Rexor's eyes were closed. All signs of life were gone. Tears streamed down Thorgrim's face. He let out a blood-curdling moan. "Aaaaauuuuuuuuuuuugghhh!"

Smoke rose to his feet and lumbered over to Sid. "You've really done it now."

"Me?"

The color returned to the rangy bounty hunter's face. "I'll be back. Make sure he doesn't go anywhere." He hustled inside the container.

Eyes fixed on the disturbing scene of one giant moaning over the other, she said, "John, where are you going?"

Smoke emerged from the container with another L.A.W. rocket. He expanded the tube and prepared it to fire.

"How many of those things did you bring?" she said.

"I always carry more than one spare." He rested the launcher on his shoulder. "Take cover."

Sid crouched behind Smoke.

Smoke yelled at the giant, "Hey, Thorgrim! Sorry about your loss. Should we send flowers or make a donation to the local giant-sized urns and crematorium? I hear they're running a two-for-one special."

Thorgrim looked up with eyes full of murder. His hands released Rexor's body.

Smoke fired.

The rocket burst from the barrel in a sizzling stream of smoke and hit dead center in the giant's gaping mouth. *Boom!* Thorgrim's head blew up like a shotgun blast through a pumpkin. Tiny hunks of giant flesh and bone showered the air. The giant headless body fell over.

Smoke discarded the rocket launching-cylinder. "Kinda cool. Kinda gross."

Standing behind him, Sid wrapped her arms around his waist. "I'll take it." Her knees buckled.

Smoke held her steady. "What's going on?"

"I took a vitamin. It's wearing off."

"Well, we aren't going to have time to lie down and take a nap. Can you make it?"

"I don't have a choice. I'm just going to have to summon all the superhero powers I have left."

"Or take another pill."

"We'll see." She surveyed the carnage. The lights were busted and hanging from the ceiling. A filmy layer of smoke rolled through the room. Bodies lay piled up to the knees in carnage. "I don't see Manson anywhere. Do you think they took him hostage?"

"I lost track of him." Smoke vanished into the container and came out with a weapons chest. He also had the Arabian sword sheathed behind his shoulders. "We'll find him or he'll find us. For now, we need to stick with the plan and disable the pyramid server. It sounded like Vormus did his part. Did you hear that explosion earlier?"

Fingering her ears as she rolled her jaw, she said, "I'm pretty sure I heard everything. Man, there's nothing worse than the sound of gunfire blasting away inside a hollow can." She dug into the weapons chest and reloaded her clips. She packed C4 into a rucksack and shouldered it. "We need to get moving."

The parking garage door opened. Men were shouting and barking orders from the other side. Sid and Smoke stepped into full view of the gap that led out into the night.

Stiff-legged deaders rushed down the ramp, followed by pea coat guards armed with guns.

Smoke raised his assault rifle and fired. The bullets tore into the dual motors of the huge garage door. The steel door dropped, crushing a deader and a man beneath it.

From one knee, Sid took aim with her rifle. She squeezed off short burst after short burst. The bullets ripped through the chests of two deaders. They dropped, flopped, and lay still. The next pair of bullets pierced the brains of the last two pea coats. "That's the last of them," she said. The barrel of her gun smoked. The enemy's hands were at the bottom of the garage door, lifting it again. She sent a spray of bullets their way. The door dropped on the bodies. Painful howls came from the other side. "They're going to keep coming. We need to get going. What are you doing?"

Smoke was down on a knee, taping a cluster of stun grenades together. "I'm making a gizmo."

"Like a MacGyver gizmo?"

"Sort of, but mine is just a tad deadlier than the Comet-and-peroxide bombs he mixes." He uncoiled some tripwire, attached it to the pins on the grenades, and wedged the cluster bomb between some bodies. "Come on."

They entered the stairwell just as the garage door opened again. A surge of men and deaders rushed into the room. Smoke and Sid took cover behind the fire exit door. Bullets riddled the metal door. Lead smashed through the door's safety glass. The guards and deaders hustled down the ramp, pointing and firing. They stepped over the cluster bomb.

"Perfect," Smoke said. He yanked the trip wire. Nothing happened. He looked at Sid and said in a Marvin the Martian voice, "Where's the kaboom? There's supposed to be an earth-shattering kaboom."

The enemy charged right at them.

CHAPTER 30

H UNKERED DOWN BESIDE SMOKE, SID pulled the pin from a hand grenade. "Here, try this."

A broad smile crossed Smoke's lips. "Aw, how did you know this was exactly what I wanted?" He cracked open the door and yelled, "Did somebody order a pineapple?" He flipped it out and closed the door.

The grenade exploded.

Boom! Kaboom! Kaboom! Kaboom!

"Ah, there's the earth-shattering kaboom." Smoke said. "It just needed a little nudging."

Sid couldn't see anything but smoke through the narrow glass window. "We need to go."

"After you."

There were three options: Upstairs, through a door into the basement, or downstairs into the subbasement. Sid took the steps down. According to Manson, that was where the main server was that needed to be destroyed. They made it down one level. The stairwell ended at another fire door.

Smoke opened the door.

Sid did a head check into the hallway. "Clear."

They slipped into the corridor. Only the emergency and exit lights illuminated the hall, which went straight about fifty feet and then crossed at a four-way intersection. Nothing aside from them stirred.

"It's feeling a little stuffy," Sid said.

Smoke held his hand up to a return air vent. "I believe Vormus actually did his job. How surprising."

"And you said never to trust a shifter."

"I still don't."

On cats' feet, they hustled down the hallway. Halfway down it were two doors, one across from the other. The doors weren't marked, and they required security access. According to Manson, the server should be in the western corner, the farthest from the garage.

Smoke lingered by the first door they came to.

"The server is this way," Sid said.

"We need to go in here."

"Why?"

"Because they'll be expecting us in the server room."

Looking at the door Smoke wanted to enter, she said, "Maybe they're expecting us in this room."

"Humor me." He pointed his weapon at the door.

Sid shoved his gun aside. "We don't have to blow up everything. Geez, I thought you were sneakier than that." She dangled an access card in front of his eyes. "See? Sneaky."

"Where'd you get that?"

"I lifted it from Samone when I dislocated her arm." She scanned the card. The security light went from red to green. "After you."

Inside was a network of huge floor-to-ceiling metal

pipes. The pipes were sweaty, and the room was filled with a suffocating humidity.

Smoke snuck through the steam. He grabbed the wheel handle on one of the valves and turned it counterclockwise. He did the same with several others. Coming back to Sid, he said, "It's going to get hot in here. It's going to get hot everywhere."

She wiped the sweat from her brow with her fingertips and opened the door across from the one they had just entered. "Oh my."

Smoke stuck his head in the door. "Ditto."

Rows of living bodies lay sunken in metal carts. The lights were low and throbbing with the rhythm of a heartbeat. The people lay in pools of a transparent golden fluid. Their faces were connected to breathing apparatus. Limbs were hooked up to strange I.V. bags. The macabre lab pulsated with weird glowing tubes, and wires ran in coils that stretched up to the ceiling like snakes.

Smoke and Sid inspected the rows.

There were dozens of bodies ranging from heavyset men to petite women. Eyes closed, their features were unlively. She studied face after face with her stomach in knots. "This is sick, Smoke."

Smoke's hard stare was focused on one of the bodies. "Sicker than you think."

His dark tone brought her toward him. "What's wrong? Is it someone we know?"

"Afraid so."

She glanced down. It was hard to make out the face on account of all the slime, but suddenly it became crystal clear. She let out a sharp gasp.

CHAPTER 31

I T WAS HER OLD FBI director and friend Ted Howard.
Sid's body went numb. "I buried him, Smoke.
I mourned with his family." She stuck her hand in
the goo. "I can feel his heart beating. Dammit!" Tears
streamed down her face. "I can't take much more of this
maddening world!"

Smoke took her by the waist and pulled her to him.
Holding her tight, he said, "I know what you mean. But
Sid, they're alive."

"They're attached to some sick and twisted machine."
She forced herself out of Smoke's hands so she could go
up and down the rows searching all the faces. She found
Asia's face half buried in the goo. "It's Asia."

"Mal will be thrilled."

Gathering herself, Sid said, "I kinda like her quiet
like this. She's so peaceful." She made her way down
one row after the other, noting a few more faces she
knew. One was an FBI agent whose name she forgot.
Another was a female news anchor from television. She

discovered the face of another man she knew all too well. "It's Senator Wilhelm."

From across the room, Smoke said, "Yeah, and he's not the only senator here."

"Are you serious? No wonder this country's leadership is so screwed up." She glared at Wilhelm. She hated the man and his son on account of all they had done to her sister. But that relationship had been going on for a long time. *How long has this madness been going on?* "We need to find Manson."

"We need to shut down the server," Smoke said. His gaze was fixed on another body. "Oh man."

Stooped over Wilhelm, Sid leaned back. "What?"

With his palms on the table, Smoke said, "It's Rebecca Lang."

"No way." Sid walked over for a look. It was the petite woman, covered from head to toe in the goo. "But last time we saw her, she was pregnant."

"There's no bulge in her belly now," Smoke said. "A pregnant clone. Now that's weird."

"At least now we know why she's always been such a pain in the ass."

Looking at all the odd wiring that covered the room like modern webbing, Sid slung some goo from her hand. "This reminds me of that scene in *The Matrix*. We've got to get them unplugged."

The main lights flickered on.

"That would be to their peril," a voice said.

Sid and Smoke whirled. Titus Tolliver, in full gargoyle form, stood in the doorway adjacent to the one they came in. The husky creature had a triumphant look on his face. "They are in a fragile state. If you do anything to change it, you will kill them."

"Maybe they'd rather be dead," Smoke said. "I figure we'd be doing them a favor."

The gargoyle slunk deeper into the room. He dipped his stony fingers into one of the patients' pools. The demon-faced man glowered at Smoke. "You don't want to play God with their lives, do you, Mister Smoke? I thought you wanted to saves lives, not take them."

"Anything is better than leaving them in your hands," Smoke said. "I'll take my chances with my maker."

Titus shrugged his brawny shoulders. His approach was slow and steady. "You might just be meeting your maker sooner than you think." He kept coming right at them.

Smoke and Sid backed toward the door they came in.

She lowered her weapon. The last thing she wanted to do was hit these people with friendly fire. Judging by the look in Titus's eyes, he was here to kill her and Smoke if he couldn't take them down. Using Smoke as a shield, she turned to back out the door. Taking a peek, she saw that the hallway was empty. Suddenly her arms and legs tired out. She felt like the only thing keeping her together was the sweetheart suit. Shoulders sagging, it was all she could do to take a breath. The supervitamin's effect had completely worn off. The adrenaline that had gotten her this far was gone too. She just wanted to sleep.

"Where are you going?" Titus said. He followed them out into the hallway. "I thought we were having a friendly conversation." He closed the door behind him.

Holding his finger to his lips he said, "Ssssh! We don't want to wake them."

"You talk too much for a gargoyle." Smoke put his assault rifle up to his shoulder and took aim. "I put you down last time with these bullets. Take one more step and I'll do the same."

Titus waggled his finger. "You caught me off guard last time. It won't happen again. My skin is impenetrable." He shrugged. "Besides, you should know I cannot die."

"That's what the giants thought. Did you see what's left of them?" Sid said.

"I'm not one to look back. I'm forward thinking." Titus stepped forward.

Smoke squeezed off two single shots in rapid succession. The concussive force of the exploding rounds shook the walls and flickered the lights.

Titus still stood. A grin formed on his big-eared, broad-nosed face. "You see? I was ready. I am ready for anything. Gargoyles, attack!"

A bat-like screech echoed down the hall. Small gargoyles rounded the corner behind them. The two-foot-high monsters raced toward Sid and Smoke on foot and with wings.

"I'll take the big one, you take the small ones!" Smoke said.

Exhausted, Sid wheeled her weapon around and started shooting out a spray of ammo. The bullets ripped through the first wave of gargoyles, blasting through their screaming bodies and blowing them up like pottery. She blasted off their rage-riddled faces. Bullets tore through legs, wings, and bodies.

A gargoyle hopped at her on one good leg.

With her weapon, she turned it to powder.

Still they came. High and low they attacked.

They latched onto her ankles. A small, hard fist smote the back of her head. One of the little monsters rode on her shoulders, pulling her hair. Using the butt of her weapon, she cracked the ones on her legs in the skulls. Noses and ears came off.

How do these things live? It's impossible.

The monsters swarmed her. They attached themselves with clawed fingers and toes, blanketing her like a net. She sagged under the great weight. They bit, struck, and clawed. With a growl, she rammed the ones she could into the wall but went down in a sea of flesh-rending gargoyle grey.

CHAPTER 32

SMOKE UNLOADED THE ENTIRE CLIP of bullets into Titus in a cadence of tiny explosions.

The gargoyle man stumbled backward on his heels and fell to the floor, then rose with a nasty look and dusted off his burly chest. "That made for quite the finale, Mister Smoke. Too bad it did not have the climax you hoped for." He stormed through the white vapors.

Chucking the weapon aside, Smoke drew one of the special knives from its sheath. He'd fought the gargoyle once before and almost died. Now he had to match the juggernaut in even more confined quarters. He needed to find its weakness.

Titus lashed out with his clawed hands.

Smoke ducked. Striking fast, he jabbed the special blade at the gargoyle's ribs. The blade slid in deep, drawing forth a howl.

Titus staggered backward holding his side. "You wounded me! You wounded me! You've found my weakness. It's my ribs! Oh, the pain! The suffering! The anguish!"

Smoke backed off, watching the gargoyle with wary eyes. "You aren't really hurt, are you."

Titus pulled the knife out with a smile, tossed it aside. "Of course not. I'm the total package."

"True, but Arabian steel can cut your skin."

"It can cut, but it can't kill. You see, I don't bleed, Mister Smoke." He punched his fist into his hand. "But you can, and you will. I'm going to turn your body and that suit you treasure into a bag of bloody smashed potatoes. I can't wait to make your bones snap and pop."

Smoke removed the sword strapped to his back. "Don't forget crackle."

Titus's eyes narrowed on the sword. "Where did you get that?"

"It's a little something I picked up at the gargoyle killer thrift shop." He spun the blade in his hands. The balance was perfect, the edge keen. He drew it two-handed to his chest. "And they even gave me the riddle steel for free."

"You're a fool if you think that blade can stop me."

"Not the blade, but the hand that wields it."

"Shut up!" Titus charged.

Smoke went into a zone. Springing forward with the sword, he chopped down hard. The blade removed Titus's right arm at the elbow.

The gargoyle barreled into Smoke like a charging bull, knocking him to the floor. Titus hammered away with his good hand. His heavy punches rocked Smoke's body.

Smoke clocked Titus in the chin with his knee and squirmed free. He popped up on his feet.

Titus rose up in a deadly crouch.

Smoke hacked into him like a berserker. The heavy blade carved into the gargoyle. Hunks of stony flesh flew. Smoke kept swinging.

Titus surged into him like a force of nature.

Both man and monster were in a maddened state of battle.

The Arabian steel sawed through Titus in another arc. A nasty strike split his skull down to the nose. Smoke ripped the steel free.

Punching at Smoke with powerful stabs, Titus said in defiance, "You cannot kill me."

"We'll see!" Smoke tore into the beleaguered gargoyle with a chop that split his knee.

Titus stumbled to the floor. Helpless agony filled his face. "No," he pleaded. He shielded his head with his arms. "Stop!"

Smoke didn't relent. With both hands he brought he sword down hard and quick.

Chop! Chop! Chop!

The gargoyle shifter had nothing left to fight with. He glared at Smoke. "I hate mortals!"

"Then I won't keep your dead brother waiting." Smoke turned the sword loose for a final blow. The blade whistled through the air.

Titus's head rolled from his shoulders. It bounced off the floor and rolled across the room before it lay still.

The smaller gargoyles collapsed all around Sid, and she lay with her face covered by her arms but bleeding. She kicked the inanimate stone monsters away. "Get off me!"

Smoke rushed over, dropped the sword, and took her by the hand. "It's over."

She fought against him.

He held her fast. "Sid, it's me."

Her eyes found his face. "Is he dead?"

"I think we're getting the hang of killing them." He moved aside, revealing Titus's body. The monster had transformed back into a man that didn't bleed so much as ooze. He combed her hair back from her eyes. "Can you move?"

"Barely. Help me up."

Smoke complied. Sid was about as banged up as he'd ever seen her. She had bad scratches all over her face. Her lip was split, and blood dripped from her chin. "Lean on me if you need to."

"No." She checked her weapons, filling her hands with two pistols. She limped down the hall. "Let's find the damn server and blow the hell out of it." She passed through the intersection, made it to the next door, and scanned the card.

Smoke opened the door. It was the electrical room, steel panels locked up with heavy padlocks. "Looks like you found home base for the electric, fire, and security systems.

"Shoot it. Shoot it all." She fired.

Smoke fired.

Bullets tore through steel. Alarms and lights went on and then out.

Smoke eased inside and set a charge of C4 along the largest conduit he could find. He hustled back out and closed the door. "Get down."

They both crouched.

Smoke triggered the detonator, unleashing a tremendous *boom*. All the lights went out.

"I'd love to go to sleep in this dark, hot mess," Sid said. The emergency and exit lights came on. "How cozy."

"They've got a backup generator running somewhere. I can hear the hum, but those emergency lights are on battery power."

Sid crawled over to the next door. The security keypad lights were still on. She scanned the card and went through the door. Icy air greeted her like the coming winter. "Morning glory, feels good." She and Smoke spilled inside. "Man, look at that thing."

Behind a ten-foot-high Plexiglas shield sat a huge computer server shaped like a pyramid. It was at least ten feet square at the base and stood ten feet high at the top. It was black with brilliant illuminating circuitry that coursed through tight veins of pulsating energy. The colors varied and changed, pulsating to a beat like the heart inside a titan's body.

Smoke made his way over to a control center that stood inside the massive room all by itself. The fifty-inch computer screen showed black. He pecked at the keyboard and shuffled the mouse. A moving image popped up on the screen. It was Kane and Allison. The burly blond man with long curls in his stringy hair had a smirk on his face. Allison appeared as voluptuous as ever in her skintight navy bodysuit.

"Hello," Kane said. "I see you made it to the server room. Well done. As you can see, the server room can be very chilly. 'Course, those elements aren't any concern for the likes of us. Hot or cold, it doesn't matter. And as you can see, the server is operating just fine. You blew up the wrong targets."

Smoke heard the door they came in latch shut.

"Oh, and the card you used to get in won't let you back out." Kane chuckled. "It's good to see you again, Sidney, but you're not looking so well. You look like you need to cool off."

An icy mist sprayed out of the sprinkler system that hung above them.

"Enjoy your hibernation, John and Sidney Smoke. Perhaps a few years in suspended animation will be enough time to let you think about things. In the meantime, your clones will be quite useful in the continuance of our operation. Good night." The screen went black.

"Man, I hate that guy," Sid said with a shiver.

Smoke yawned. His eyes became heavy. His vision blurred. He said in forced speech, "All of a sudden I feel like the Cowardly Lion in the field outside the Emerald City."

CHAPTER 33

S ID TOTTERED ON HER FEET and bumped into Smoke.

He steadied her by holding her beneath her armpits. "Do you know how to clear a gas mask?"

"What?" she said with her head drooping over her shoulders. Her eyelids were drooping, too.

In Smoke's long fingers were a pair of black breathing apparatuses, something like what you'd see in an airplane. He stretched the black surgical cords over her head and snapped the cup over her mouth. He stuck another apparatus over his head, covering his mouth and nose, saying, "Breathe out! Breathe out!" He covered the filters on his mask and, blinking really hard, he exhaled.

Sid fell on the floor, staring up at the ceiling.

I don't want to breathe out. I just want to sleep.

A blurry Smoke leaned over her and attached something to her mask.

As she breathed in short gasps, her languid lungs came to life. The image of Smoke's face sharpened as she sucked in more mouthfuls of air.

Smoke took her by the arm and sat her up. He gave her a firm shake. "Sorry, hun, naptime is over. They think we're asleep. Now's the time to move."

The mist stopped spraying out of the sprinklers.

"Just get me up to my feet," she said. With Smoke's assistance, she finally made it back up. Her arms and legs burned with pins and needles. She shook them. "You didn't regurgitate this mask, did you?"

"No comment." He pulled his mask away from his face and sniffed the air.

"What are you doing?" She tried to shove the mask back onto his face.

"It's clear now." He wiped his nose. "It smells a little funny though." Using the mask, he covered the camera mounted on top of the monitor Kane had spoken from earlier and turned his attention to the pyramid server. From his satchel, he took out block after block of C4 and set them on the desk. "We need to plant this stuff before they show up."

Sid hit the Plexiglas wall that protected the server. It didn't even shudder. "Don't you think it's indestructible? It's inches thick."

"These shifters say everything is indestructible," Smoke said, slapping the C4 into the seams where the glass met with the concrete ceiling, "but the only indestructible thing I know of in this world is my love for you."

Sid stopped what she was doing, and with a smile she said, "Aw, how sweet. Moments like this remind me why I so enjoy blowing things up with you."

Smoke chuckled. With a fierce grin, he attached a

disk the size of his fist to the glass in the center of the four charges he had set. He depressed a button. A tiny yellow light flared, and the disc let out a charging whine.

"What is that?" Sid said.

"It's a sonic disrupter. It sends high-frequency sound waves into the glass. It works like a tuning fork. It's not powerful enough to shatter the glass on its own, but hopefully it will weaken the structure just enough for the nasty plastique to do the rest."

Nodding, she said, "I like it. You think of everything."

Smoke stuck the detonation caps into the C4. "Yeah, well, they're overconfident. That's their weakness to exploit."

"And what's your weakness?" she said, taking him by the waist and digging her nails into his ribs. Sid didn't know why she did it, but she tried to tickle him. For some reason, Smoke was driving her crazy right now. The ease and purpose with which he moved made her heart flutter. "Am I your weakness?"

"No, you're my strength." He squeezed her hand in his as he stared at his handiwork. "That ought to do it."

The security latches on the doors to the room popped.

"Time to play possum," he said, crouching on the floor.

"You like this game entirely too much," she said, lowering herself. "Why don't we just beat the crap out of the pea coats when they come?"

Smoke shrugged. "The lady makes the call."

Together they hid out of sight behind the computer station and waited. Within a minute the door and the one adjacent to it opened. Sid could see a pair of pea coats armed with machine guns slip into the room, their hard eyes searching the floor. She pointed in the direction of the two she could see.

Smoke nodded.

Weapons ready, they popped up from behind the computer console and fired off two quick shots.

Two guards dropped dead with bullet holes in their heads.

"Status report?" said a voice on the radio gripped in one guard's hand.

Smoke glided over and picked it up. "All secure. We have the persons detained." He smiled at Sid.

She could see playfulness come to life in his eyes. "Don't, Smoke."

"Also," Smoke continued, "One of the prisoners is really hot. Can you check her marital status? I'm not having much luck on my Matchmaker account."

The voice came over the radio. "Who is this?"

Silently, Sid mouthed the words to Smoke, "Don't say it."

In a rugged voice, he replied in the radio, "I'm Batman." He chucked the radio aside and resumed his normal voice. "Let's go."

Live video of Kane and Allison appeared on the monitor again. Their faces were filled with curiosity as their eyes scanned the room.

Smoke removed the gas mask from the camera and waved at them. "Hi!"

Sid popped her head in. "Hey!"

Together they waved.

Smoke turned the computer camera around, facing

the server. He backed up and pointed to the C4. "You might want to cover those big ears of yours, Kane, because your server is about to go boom. Bye bye now!"

Kane's eyebrows knitted.

Smoke and Sid left the images of Kane and Allison screaming at the top of their lungs and hustled out of the room. They sprinted down the corridor, made a turn around the intersection, stopped, and turned.

Smoke held up the detonator. "Would you like to have the honor?"

She grabbed his hand in hers. "Let's do it together."

They hit the switch.

Boom!

CHAPTER 34

SID WALKED OVER THE INTERIOR carnage that lay on the floor. Her boots crunched over stone. The pyramid server room was toast. The walls were bowed out. The drywall was dust. The doors had been blown from their hinges. Every speck of organization had been erased. The charred cement ceiling crumbled. The center computer console had become nothing but scrap and microbits.

The only things standing were the server and the clear wall surrounding it.

The clear finish of the glass was blackened by scorch marks, but it stood. The glass had cracked all over with spidery veins from top to bottom. She could still see the server glowing with life on the other side.

"I can't believe it," she said as she felt her heart deflate.

"Don't believe everything you see." Smoke walked up to the shield glass and poked it with his finger. Fragments of glass fell like frosty snowflakes.

Chin up, Sid moved forward and hit the glass wall

with the butt of her handgun. The glass dropped in larger ice-like chunks. "Screw this," she said, checking her weapon's clip. It was filled with blue-tipped bullets. "Back up."

"You're the boss," Smoke said, stepping aside with a grin.

Sid blasted a ring of bullets the size of her head through the glass. With a kick, she knocked the circle of glass out. Looking up at Smoke, she said, "Got any more—"

"Pineapples?" Smoke handed her two grenades. She pulled the pins and tossed them through the hole. She and Smoke took cover behind a long stretch of board that had been part of the computer console. "This better do it."

A muffled *boom* was followed by the tinkling of shattering glass.

Rising from behind their protection, Sid could see the pyramid server burning.

The pulsating lights of its living network went out. The entire building fell silent. It was as if the heartbeat of the building had stopped.

Sid rested her forehead on Smoke's shoulder. "Finally. Whew! I didn't think we would ever kill that thing."

"Huh, I was starting to doubt it too."

"We need to go check on Ted and the others." She ran out of the room, down the hall, and back into the laboratory. Many bodies shuddered inside the bounds. A gaunt figure had his back to Sid.

"Hey!" she said, firing a warning shot. "Hands where I can see them! Get away from there!"

"I'm reaching for the sky," the man said as he slowly turned. It was Vormus. "Is this high enough?"

"Just back away," she said.

Manson appeared from behind Vormus. He was the blond-headed, blue-eyed boy again. With restless energy, he said, "We have to disconnect all of them now! Yank every cord and breathing apparatus you can find. Without the computer giving the orders, their bodies will shut down and die." He yanked the tube out of one man's mouth and plucked the cables connected to the man's head. "Their bodies need to awaken!"

On a motherly instinct more than following orders, Sid did as requested. She went from body to body, yanking out the slimy tubes and macabre wiring. She found Asia and set her free, saying, "Asia, wake up."

All the little woman did was blink.

Smoke entered and did the same. Many of the people coughed and sputtered. Some convulsed. "This one looks like she's having a heart attack." It was Rebecca Lang. "What do I do?"

"Nothing," Manson said with his head down at the task at hand. "There's no guarantee they can adjust to the real world again. Just keep doing what you're doing."

Sid kept at it. She caught Smoke's eye.

His face was stern. He said to her with a quick nod, "Survivors survive."

Finally she was at Ted Howard's cart, and she removed the breathing tube from his mouth. Her quick hands pulled the needles from his head. "Oh, Ted," she said, holding his cheek.

The husky man's body trembled. He shook the cart

so hard it scraped over the floor. His chest jumped. He coughed and hacked. His forearms strained against his restraints.

"Manson! Get over here! This is bad! None of the others resisted like this."

Manson hopped clear over a table and landed right beside her. He stuck his hands in the goo and cupped Ted's straining neck. "Oh my, this isn't good. I believe he actually is in cardiac arrest." He shrugged. "Sorry, Sid, it happens."

"Sorry my ass!" Sid shoved Manson to the floor. Immediately she started giving Ted chest compressions. "Come on, Ted, Come on! You can't die on me now!"

Ted's body went still.

"Nooo!" she screamed. She kept pressing on his chest. After all this time, she couldn't believe Ted was still alive.

The one who died must have been a clone!

It had hurt so much when she'd lost him the last time that she couldn't stand to lose him again. "Ted, your family needs you! I need you! Fight, Ted!" Tears streaming down her face, she alternated between chest compressions and mouth-to-mouth breathing.

His body didn't move.

Smoke grabbed her arm and tried to pull her away.

She shrugged him off. "No!"

Putting his strength behind it, Smoke pulled her back. "He's gone, Sid. I'm sorry."

Every last ounce of strength she had fled her. She collapsed into Smoke's chest, crying and sobbing. She pounded on his chest. "Why?"

Smoke didn't have the answer. He held her upright in his strong arms. "Let's help the others."

"I can't bury him again, John. I can't." She stared back at Ted. He lay in the table goo, lifeless as a mannequin. "No person should have to go through this. What am I supposed to say to his family?"

"So far as they know, he died with honor. I'd leave it that way."

"But that's not the truth. He died like this."

"He lived with honor. That's what matters. It's the truth."

"Let's just try one more thing, shall we?" Manson had a huge metal syringe in his hand and held it over Ted's chest. "Normally, I wouldn't do this, but somehow all this sappiness got to me. But no more blubbering if it doesn't work."

"What is that?" Sid said as she turned and wiped the tears from her eyes.

"This isn't the first time these bodies have had spasms. Every once in a while we have to reboot them. This is my version of an intracardiac injection. Lots of adrenaline. But your friend is old and has a bad heart, probably from too much chili fries and beer, so don't go harping on me if it doesn't work. He's better off dead if you ask me. How would you explain his revival?" He poised the needle over Ted's chest. "Well?"

"Do it!"

CHAPTER 35

MANSON PLUNGED THE NEEDLE INTO Ted's chest. His thumb pressed the fluid down, and Ted's body leaped parallel off the table, where it flopped like a fish out of water and steadied. His eyes were wide open. His lips mumbled.

Sid leaned over him. "Ted, it's me, Sid."

Ted spat goo. "What the hell happened? I feel like a car ran over my chest." His soft eyes darted around. "Where the hell am I?"

She said to Manson, "He's awfully alert."

"It's the adrenaline. It'll wear off. He breathes...for now."

"We need to get him out of here. We need to get them all out of here. Ted, what's the last thing you remember?"

Blinking rapidly, he said, "Eating pizza and drinking beer. Why? Did I have a heart attack? That's it, isn't it. I had a heart attack." He found Smoke looking at him. "Oh, it's you. Smoke, right? Everything's hazy." He strained against his bonds. "Why am I tied up? And why am I covered in pea soup? Sid, what's going on?"

"I'll fill you in on the way home," she said. All over the room, the awakened people began to stir. One woman fell off her cart. It was Rebecca Lang. "Manson, can they walk?"

"Not well. They haven't used their limbs in months. Some haven't moved for years. They might be awake, but I'm not certain we can just waltz them out of here. Let's not forget there's a horde of deaders and pea coats out there, wanting to rip us all apart."

"You stay here," Smoke said to Sid. "Vormus and I will check it out. Are you going to be okay?"

She nodded. "I'm not going anywhere without them."

Smoke and Vormus stood inside the garage bay. It was a war zone. Men shot to pieces. Even shifters lay still. Smoke was relieved to see that the giants—Lance, Thorgrim, and Rexor—hadn't moved at all. The only things moving aside from him and Vormus were the deaders. A handful still moved. Their foul bodies lay on the cement floor, struggling to move without the necessary limbs. Smoke finished them off with bullets to the chest.

"You sure made quite a mess," Vormus commented as he stepped over the wreckage.

"You can't clean up evil without getting messy." Before he headed up into the garage, he'd retrieved the Arabian sword and put it back in its sheath. He slid it out again.

Vormus eyed him.

"Just a precaution," Smoke said. He ran up the ramp

that led outside into the courtyard of the compound. "Let's go."

The only thing stirring outside was the wind. The guard shack was abandoned, the gate wide open. A fire burned on the rooftop. Smoke did a three-sixty. There had been several cars and trucks in the lot, but now they were gone. Only one single black SUV remained, parked in the front.

"Do you think Kane left?"

Vormus shrugged. "It's hard to say. He's a stubborn man." His eye caught something moving inside the building.

Smoke turned.

A man walked through the glass doors and down the steps. His nice shirt and slacks were torn up. A cigarette burned between his fingers. Half of Reginald's face looked like it had been skinned off. "Pardon the appearance, but explosions tend to do that. An angry Kane does, too." His skin was repairing itself, his svelte look slowly returning. "I've got a message for you. Kane's pissed."

CHAPTER 36

R EGINALD CHUCKLED. "MY, I'VE NEVER seen Kane so angry. You know, that's a rare thing when you make a shifter angry. Normally, our polished resolve does not come unfettered, but today, well, things got ugly."

"So, are you here to congratulate us?" Smoke asked. "Is there going to be a trophy ceremony?"

"Such a clever tongue, Smoke." Reginald flicked off the ashes of his cigarette. "It's that stand-up routine I like about you. But no, you won't be getting any kind of trophy for your achievement. But I have to admit, I never thought you would be able to take that server down. Your fortitude is incredible. Kane literally jumped up and down screaming when the pyramid exploded. I found it amusing, myself." Keeping his distance from his adversaries, he walked over to a light pole and leaned against it. He lit another cigarette. "You managed to wreck decades of work—in an extremely bold move, I might add. 'Course, you had some unique help." He eyed Vormus.

"Changing sides gave my hollow life a dash of flavor," Vormus replied.

"Vormus, you can't undo what you've done. You know that. He's just leading you along, Smoke. That leopard won't change his spots. Once his zeal for entertainment is over, he'll come back to the brood. This isn't the first time he's tried something like this, you know. He did the same thing with Guermo."

Smoke gave Vormus a look. He didn't trust the shifter as far as he could throw him, and he always watched his back. He wouldn't be one bit surprised if Vormus turned on him at any moment. He focused back on Reginald. "So what's the end game? If there's no trophy, then why are you here?"

Reginald puffed out a smoke ring. "To kill you. To kill you both."

"You against us?" Smoke said. He tapped the tip of his sword on the pavement. "I like those odds. I've developed a knack for killing shifters."

"Yes, you have conquered many. Kudos to you. But no, I don't plan to battle you in a melee contest. It's your soul I want to slay." Reginald pushed off the lamppost. "You see, you actually have achieved something quite devastating. You wiped out the clones. Oh, I can't imagine the horror that has erupted all over DC. Just think about it. All of the clones that have been so carefully planted out there have lost their connection to the computer."

He removed a phone from his pocket and eyed the screen. "These little things have made our jobs so much easier. Hah! Listen to these headlines." He cleared his throat. "Mayor Roslyn's speech turns into a babbling nightmare. Police Chief Bannon drops dead. Congressman Agnew races naked in the streets. Oh, a streaker. Now that's funny, but hardly anything shocking from the political ilk. But eh. Just you wait and see, all this current news popping up tonight will be wiped clean tomorrow. Don't you understand, mortal? *WE* control everything. The secret wars we fight have been witnessed by countless eyes, yet the truth is still hidden from the public. You might win one battle, but in the end, you're still going to lose the war. The Drake always wins."

Smoke stepped forward. "You didn't win tonight."

"Don't hoist your trophy up over your head so soon, Smoke. Even though you've proven you have a knack for being one step ahead in most things, you'll never be a step ahead in everything. We aren't so overconfident that we lack a contingency plan." He held out his phone. "As you can see, I have a phone, and with this phone I can do many things. I can call Kane. Order pizza. Play a mind-numbing game. Or I can detonate explosives. You're familiar with explosives, aren't you? Why yes you are. You've been blowing up a lot of things." Reginald pecked on the screen. "But we have bombs in place as well. You see, if the operation of the Drake were ever discovered, we would have to destroy all evidence. So it's armed with explosives."

"You're bluffing."

"No, I'm not. If your little helper Manson was as smart as he thought, he would have known this entire facility could be detonated from outside. You didn't have to smash in here like a bunch of angry pirates. You could have used some sophistication." He flicked his cigarette away. "Anyhow, the entire roomful of people you rescued are nothing but hostages now. That goes for your wife and all her precious friends." He shrugged. "Now, there's a remote chance she'll survive the explosion with the suit on, but I don't think she or anyone else will make it out when the building collapses right on top of them. It will be a crushing defeat."

"I will finish you one way or the other."

"You're perfectly fine with all those people dying when you could save them?" Reginald hitched up a brow. "No, you couldn't live with it. Just imagine the thought of never seeing your wife alive again. No more hugs. No kisses. No making love at the beach. The very love of your life buried in one of the heaviest tombs ever. How sad."

Smoke's fingers twitched. His grip on the sword tightened.

Reginald continued as he paced with an easy stride. "And think about your baby. You'll never get to hold your baby."

"What are you talking about now?"

"Oh, what a surprise, the man with an uncanny ability to be a step ahead of everything doesn't know his own wife is pregnant? Perhaps she doesn't want you to know. How interesting. Perhaps because it's not your baby. Perhaps it's Kane's."

Smoke had his suspicions to begin with. Sid had shown signs of morning sickness several times. "If the child is Kane's, I don't think he would want to see the baby in the grave."

"That's where you're wrong. Kane's sired many, and

they're all dead. Typically, neither the woman nor the baby survives the birthing process. If they did, shifters would be everywhere. Wouldn't that be glorious?"

"Is this true?" he said to Vormus.

"Neither of us have any children."

According to Manson, Vormus, and Mal, the shifters couldn't breed with each other, but every once in a while a female shifter would be impregnated by a mortal male. In rare cases the baby could survive. That was the theory behind Smoke and Sid, that they were shifter offspring. The thought of his mother or Sid's mother being a shifter made him sick. "What do you want, Reginald? Or rather, what does Kane want?"

"Surrender and come with me, willingly, to meet Kane."

"And if I don't?"

Reginald held up the phone. "Then your family dies."

CHAPTER 37

SURRENDER. IT WASN'T EVER PART of Smoke's modus operandi. He set the sword on the ground. "I agree, but I want to see everyone out safely first."

"But. Such a troublesome word. But—just this once—I'll reward it in good faith." Reginald gave a sharp whistle. Nestled in the hedges that hugged the building was Swift Venison the were-rat. He slipped out of the bushes wearing nothing but a pair of pants. His fuzzy chest and arms rippled with knots of muscle. He slinked beside Reginald, wringing his pinkish, long-nailed hands. "What is your bidding?"

"Make sure he doesn't have a weapon on him. Vormus, step aside."

Vormus complied.

Venison padded over. With eyes like coal orbs, he picked over Smoke's body, removing the gear belt and, before tossing it aside, snapping on a pair of flex cuffs. "I hate these things." He secured Smoke's hands crossed behind his back with the cuffs. He pulled them tight.

Smoke winced.

Venison touched Smoke's cold ear with his nose. "Uncomfortable, isn't it?"

Smoke lifted his shoulders.

The were-rat shoved Smoke's head aside, reached down, and picked up the sword. He brought the edge to Smoke's throat. "If it were up to me, I'd be done with you. One swing and I'd turn your head into a bloody kickball."

"That's enough, Venison," Reginald warned. "Kane doesn't want him harmed. Maybe roughed up a bit."

"Roughed up?" Venison clacked his teeth together really fast. His long whiskers brushed Smoke's cheek. "Thanks to you, I was stuck in the hole!" He cocked back his elbow and punched Smoke in the gut. The blow lifted Smoke up on his toes.

Smoke groaned. "You hit awfully hard for a rat. A girl rat."

Venison's tail coiled around Smoke's neck and squeezed his face red.

"That's enough!" Reginald ordered. "Just pat him down and take him to the car. Buckle him into the front seat and keep a gun on his head." He turned his attention to Vormus. "Go ahead and fetch your friends."

Chin up and eyes down on Reginald, Vormus floated away with a sneer and vanished into the garage.

Smoke took a seat in the car. The leather squeaked under him.

Venison buckled him in. He kept the gun barrel on Smoke's temple. "Just give me a reason. Any reason at all. I'd love to blast a tunnel through your head."

"And I'd still have more between my ears than you do

now, rat. Tell me, why'd you choose to be a rat? Was it a natural affection for waste and filth?"

Venison peeked over at Reginald. He was on the phone with his back turned. Venison punched Smoke in the jaw. "Shut up!"

The were-rat walked around the SUV and crawled into the driver's seat, started the engine, dropped the shifter into drive, and pulled up alongside Reginald, hitching his elbow out the window. "We've got them now. Just blow the rest up. Kane won't be mad. If anything, he'll be glad."

"Don't be an imbecile, Venison. Now turn the car around so she can get a good look at him."

As soon as Vormus entered the room, Sid said, "Where's Smoke?"

"He's outside with Reginald."

"Reginald!" She rushed toward the doors.

Vormus blocked her exit.

She stuck a gun in his face. "Get out of my way!"

"At least let me tell you what to expect."

"I'll pass."

"I insist. Apparently, this building is set for detonation. Reginald holds the trigger. In exchange for your safety and everyone else's, Smoke agreed to become Kane's prisoner."

"No! I'm not letting that happen."

"It's too late," Vormus said. "Your husband made his decision. If he's not gone yet, he'll be gone as soon as you get there. I recommend you stay here. Kane won't kill you, but he'll backtrack and kill the rest of them." He eyed the people stirring in their troughs of goo. Many of them were sitting up and talking.

Manson eyed the ceiling. "You don't want all that blood on your hands."

Sid took a quick glance back. She shook her head. "No, I've got to see him."

Vormus stepped aside.

Sid raced away.

He said to Manson as he eyeballed the ceiling, "Do you really think this entire building is wired to explode?"

"That's what I would do."

"Then why aren't you running?"

"I'm staying with them," said the man in the child's body. "There are worse ways to go. But I don't know what you're standing around for. Someone needs to protect her."

Sid's long legs ached with every stride. She'd never felt so tired in her life. She pushed up the incline and passed under the ruined inner garage door, which was propped open with a ladder. The short sprint left her winded as she reached the top of the driveway. Hands on hips and sucking for breath, she saw Reginald standing beside the SUV.

Smoke sat in the passenger seat. He winked at her. "Hi, honey."

She approached.

"I'm going to advise you not to come any closer, Mrs. Smoke," Reginald said.

"What's going on?"

"In exchange for your safety and that of those left in the basement, your dear husband has agreed to come with me. And if he doesn't come peacefully," he held up his phone, "boom."

"You're a bastard, Reginald!"

"Don't be upset with me. It's not my plan, it's Kane's. He's quite the control freak, and I have to tell you, you've made him very, very angry. But in the end, he will have what he wants: Smoke."

"I thought he wanted me," she said, easing forward. "Take me instead of him."

"That was the idea in the beginning, but now Kane feels you are tainted. He has a sure thing with Smoke, but there is little to gain with you, seeing how you might only have a few months left to live."

Sid stiffened. "What are you talking about?"

"Your pregnancy. It is almost certain death for a woman who becomes impregnated by a shifter." He shrugged. "One would have figured Kane would be more careful about that."

Skin crawling beneath her suit, she said with curled lips, "You're lying."

"I have no reason to lie. Besides, it was your foul copulations that got you into this mess. You should have been more careful." He opened the back door. "But enjoy today's small victory while you still live. It was quite a blow."

"Wait!"

Reginald closed the door.

"John, don't believe a word he says!"

The SUV moved forward with Smoke's eyes on hers. The window started to roll up, and Smoke said, "If he's a boy, name him after me."

"John!" She ran after the SUV all the way to the gate. The vehicle's red taillights outdistanced her and disappeared around the first bend in the road. The echo of the engine faded. She held her hand to her abdomen. The moments of her being sick rushed through her head. It all came together, and she knew her instincts were true. She dropped to her knees. "Morning glory, I'm pregnant."

CHAPTER 38

"ARE YOU OKAY?' VORMUS ASKED her.

She glanced up. The shifter with long ghostly white hair floated inches above the ground with a backdrop of black cloudy sky behind him. The wind picked up, blowing his hair. Sid's chest tightened as she soaked everything in.

"How did Reginald know I was pregnant?"

"Shifters have heightened senses. My guess is he sensed the extra heartbeat."

"Did you sense it?"

"Yes."

"And you didn't say anything?"

"I honestly didn't think you wanted to hear the news from me, did you? Wouldn't that have spoiled the moment?"

"Not nearly as bad as what Reginald just did. Bastard." With a grunt, she pushed herself up to her feet. "It can't be Kane's baby, can it? It's been too long since I've been with him."

"Shifters run off a different chemistry. It's hard to say who fertilized the condemned egg."

"Don't say that."

"Fertilized?"

"No, condemned." Her eyes followed the road. A void filled her. Smoke was gone. He had made a sacrifice to save her and everyone else. She had a sinking feeling it would be more than just his life. She could still see the window rolling up over his face. His lips were still moving.

Oh crap, he was saying something!

Stunned, she closed her eyes, envisioning the scene again. Watching his lips move over and over again in her mind, she mumbled.

"What are you doing?"

"Ssssh!"

She got it. "Get them out!"

"Get who out?"

"The people who were cloned. Oh crap, we have to get them out of there!" With a surge of new strength, she ran for the building, down the ramp, down the stairwell, and into the room.

With a bad limp, Manson was already leading the people outside. He said to Sid, "We're about to go boom, aren't we."

"I'm not taking any chances." She threw a man's arm over her shoulder and started leading him up the stairwell, yelling, "Vormus!"

Vormus appeared in the fire exit door. "Yes?"

"Help us get them all clear of the building."

"Saving mortals isn't something I'm accustomed to. Be wise and just leave before it's too late."

Standing in the garage, she said, "Really? That's funny, seeing how you aren't as immortal as you think." She pointed at the fallen giants with her chin and then shoved the man she was helping into Vormus's hands. "Everyone dies if we don't get moving."

Taking the man by the waist, he said, "I see your point, but I hardly feel threatened."

The outer garage door dropped—past the one Sid and Smoke had blasted off the motors—sealing them inside. Yellow emergency lights flashed. An alarm sounded over and over with a loud buzzing sound. A computerized female voiced counted down. "Sixty... fifty-nine...fifty-eight..."

Hand to her forehead, Sid said, "It's like a James Bond nightmare."

"James who?"

Sid spotted the shipyard container. "In there! Take the people in there!"

She got Ted to safety and then rushed up the steps with two people attached to her hips. It was like carrying sandbags. "Come on!" she said to the shifters. "You have to help me."

Vormus carried two over his shoulders.

Manson did as well, with a slightly embarrassed shrug at how weak he had tried to seem.

"...Twenty-seven...twenty six..."

Sid got the pair inside and made another run. She passed Manson on the way down. The young boy carried a girl in his arms. "How many more are there?"

"Three."

She made it into the hallway, where a man and a woman were slumped over. The man was the heavyset

Augustus Wilhelm. She took a peek into the lab and didn't see a third person inside the room.

"Dammit!" Sid hustled over to Wilhelm and the much smaller lady.

It was Rebecca Lang. She looked at Sid with lucid eyes.

Sid's jaw hung open. "Rebecca, get on my back! Wilhelm, get your sorry ass up those stairs and into the shipping container, or you're going to die!"

Blinking, he said from a sagging jaw, "Where am I?"

"You're about fifteen seconds from hell, you sonuvabitch!" She grabbed his arm. "Now get your ass up!"

Rebecca's lithe arms latched onto Sid's back. She was saying, "Thank you. Thank you."

Somehow, Sid made it up the stairs with both of them. She staggered to the container and dropped them inside.

"...nine...eight...seven..."

"I didn't see a third person down there," she said to Manson.

"I'll take care of it."

"There's no time!"

From behind, Vormus hauled her inside with a fling that sent her sprawling on top of all the others.

Manson and Vormus closed the container doors together, with Manson saying, "Goodbye, Sid." The doors shut and sealed. Her world became pitch black. Outside was the sound of the world coming to an end with a repeated ear-jolting *BOOM—BOOM—BOOM*!

CHAPTER 39

WITH A GRIN ON HIS face, Reginald set his phone down on the center console. "All in a day's work."

Venison drove, but the were-rat still had a gun in Smoke's face.

Shifting in his seat, Smoke said, "You killed them, didn't you."

"Again, to be clear, I was only following orders."

Jaws clenching, Smoke replied, "We had a deal."

"You had a deal with me, but Kane supersedes that."

"So you're supposed to be the good guy?"

"On the contrary, I'm glad to see them all go. I'm not a people person. The fewer, the better. But I'm sure your cherished bride survived. I did let her out, you know. My, I just had a thought. I hope she didn't go back inside." Reginald leaned forward. He opened the center console and fished out a hard pack of Camel unfiltered cigarettes. He tapped a cig out from the carton and put it between his lips. Reading the pack, he said, "Turkish and domestic blend. I always found that to be a unique selling point. Have you ever been to Turkey, Smoke?"

"I can't say I have."

"Well, who knows what your new future might bring." Reginald offered a cigarette. "Smoke, Smoke? We have a long ride ahead."

"Funny, but I'll pass. Those things will kill you, you know."

"So I've heard." Reginald eased into the backseat. He took a Zippo from his pocket, flicked the top open, and struck up the flame. Lighting his cigarette, he said, "I love tobacco almost as much as I love killing people. It's so... satisfying."

Venison coughed. "I think it's disgusting." He rolled down his window and checked Reginald in the rearview mirror. "A filthy mortal habit. You should be above that."

"It's my way of blending in. Now roll that window back up. It messes up my hair."

"So where are we going?" Smoke said, adding in a cough to cover the sound of his diamond-dust-peppered fingernails sawing at his flex cuffs. "Is it another secret location buried deep in the heart of DC? Personally, I think it would be cool if it was the White House. I've never been."

"You are being taken to a transformation station. Willing or not, you're going to be subjected to the change. Kane's excited to see how the shifter blood in you will respond. You might want to give a little thought to the kind of monster you want to shift into. I'm sure there is some creature out there you identify with."

Reginald stuck the cigarette pack in front of Smoke's face. "A camel, perhaps? Now that would be different."

Venison let out a high-pitched chuckle.

Still clawing at his weakening bonds, Smoke said, "How about a doppelganger? Huh? I could be your replacement."

"No one can replace me." Reginald blew a stream of yellow smoke out his nose. "I'm the top of the line."

"There's always someone better and stronger out there. You just haven't met them yet."

"I'm certain whoever it is, it isn't you." Reginald's eyes drifted to the window.

"Certainly not." Venison snickered and coughed. The gun barrel wobbled.

Smoke rolled his wrists, snapping his bonds just as they passed over a pothole. They were about a mile from the main highway. "Bumpy ride," Smoke said to Venison.

"I like the potholes. I pretend they are people." Venison aimed for a bad patch in the road. The vehicle jostled.

Smoke acted. He knocked the gun aside with one hand and jerked the car wheel with the other. The vehicle sped over the embankment, crashing through the trees. It smacked hard on its side and tumbled side over side, finally smashing hard into an oak tree. Smoke wrenched the gun free from Venison's hands, undid his seatbelt, and squeezed out of the busted car window.

As soon as he came to his feet, Venison was there, chest heaving. A nasty scrape crossed the bridge of his nose.

"You idiot! I'll kill you for what you did!"

"Not as long as I have this." Smoke held up his pistol.

Venison's rat eyes widened.

Smoke filled him with blue-tipped lead with two shots to the heart and two to the head.

Venison dropped on the spot.

Reginald appeared from the other side of the vehicle with his cigarette bent in his mouth. He was clapping. "Clever. Very clever. Another shifter bites the dust." He dropped his cigarette on Venison's face. "Eh, he always was a weak one anyway. A shot through the heart and head is rat poison to the likes of him. But now you're going to have to deal with me. That little gun of yours won't work on me."

Smoke tossed the gun aside. "I won't need it to take you down."

Reginald pushed his sleeves up. "Apparently you've forgotten the beating I gave you last time."

"No, I've been thinking about it every day."

CHAPTER 40

"Y ou're a fool, Smoke. I've honed my skills over hundreds of years." Reginald stepped over some saplings down to the open ground where the hillside bottomed out and train tracks bent through the woods. "This level ground makes for a more suitable arena. I'd rather not fight among the sticks. I'm quite fond of this shirt." He rubbed the sleeve. "It's from Italy. I like the Italians. They're very passionate people." His face changed into the image of Rocky Balboa. He hunkered down into a boxer's stance with is lazy eyes fixed on Smoke. "Come on, Apollo. Let's go."

Smoke climbed up the gravel and in between the tracks. "You just ruined one of my favorite movies."

Reginald goaded him on with large white fists. "No talk. Just fight."

Smoke stepped in. He raised his fists. "This is weird."

"Did you take your little pills, Smoke? You're going to need them."

"No pills. Just skills."

"Heh, a fatal mistake. You could have increased your

chance of survival by one percent." The doppelganger skipped in and unleashed some jabs.

Smoke slid his chin out of the way. He blocked a flurry of punches with his arms. Reginald might've been smaller than he was, but he hit like a heavyweight. Smoke absorbed the blows on his shoulders.

Reginald ducked, jabbed, and punched like Rocky on speed.

Smoke dropped and took Reginald down with a leg sweep.

The doppelganger landed hard on his back but popped right back up with his neck stretched out. "Yo! What's the deal, Smoke? Why are you fighting dirty?"

Smoke rushed in and clobbered him in the jaw. The powerful blow took Reginald off guard. His knees buckled. Smoke put his full weight on the man. He pummeled him down onto the tracks. He hit Reginald so hard his face changed.

Reginald turned from Rocky to Mister T. "Get off me, fool!"

"Shut up!" Smoke punched him in the mouth again and again.

Reginald's arms sprang into action, swatting Smoke's hammering blows aside. With a smile on his face, he said, "Are your arms getting tired yet?"

"No, but my eyes are!" Smoke drove his knuckles through Reginald's chin so hard the doppelganger changed color.

Reginald twisted out of Smoke's grasp. Like a wild hog, he scrambled away and onto his feet. When he turned, his face was back to normal. The cunning look of an English assassin returned. He spat a tooth out. "You've been thinking an awful lot."

"You had impeccable timing the last time we fought. I'd just battled two giants and didn't have much left. Made it easy for you."

"It wouldn't have made any difference one way or the other. You can't hurt me. All you'll do is tire yourself out, and when that inevitably happens, I'll pummel you to death." Somewhere an owl hooted. "There is no sweeter sound than bone busting up bone. I'm personally fond of the sound when the jaw gives. It has such a quieting effect."

"Thanks for the suggestion." Smoke waded in and threw a series of punches and kicks.

Reginald blocked and countered.

With every punch Smoke made, Reginald came back even quicker. Smoke's uncanny knack for avoiding movement before it started saved him from getting knocked senseless. It was that special ability that made him wonder if there truly was shifter blood in him. He had no choice but to embrace it now. It was survival. Instinct.

Reginald popped him in the lips with a backfist. "You're bleeding, Smoke. That fragile shell of yours cracks."

Smoke took a quick breath. His lungs burned. He went at Reginald again, using his longer reach to keep the quicker man at bay. He feinted with a rib jab, pulled it, and countered with a hard southpaw uppercut. His fist connected with jaw.

The blow lifted Reginald up on his toes. His eyes widened.

Smoke locked up the man's head. He drove the punches home. Ribs cracked. He laid into the shifter with everything he had, one nasty Rocky punch after another.

The shifter slipped out of Smoke's grip and stumbled over the track, collapsing on the ground. Reginald was down on his knees, huffing, with a hand stuck down in the gravel. He leered at Smoke. His eyebrows knitted. "I'm tired of toying with you." He transformed. His body filled out his loose-fitting clothes. "Let's see how you do against this."

Staring down at an image of himself, Smoke wiped the blood from his lip. "You've never looked better, Reginald." He gave his other self an approving nod. "I look mighty fine in those Italian duds."

"Oh, shut up." Reginald climbed up the railway track. "Better yet, I'm going to shut you up."

As soon as Reginald stepped over the first track, Smoke launched some furious punches.

Reginald deflected them with big hands and fluid tae kwon do moves.

Smoke changed tactics. He delivered a fierce kick to Reginald's crotch.

The doppelganger moaned.

Smoke winced. "That sort of hurt me to do that."

Reginald caught the next kick. He pulled Smoke to the ground.

They wrestled over the tracks in an angry tangle of muscle. In combinations of well-executed judo moves, the tussle banged heads and limbs off the metal rails.

Fists smacked hard into jaws and faces. Elbows jabbed ribs. Chins tasted knuckles.

Smoke fought like a lion against this stronger and quicker version of himself. His sharp mind sensed every move before it happened, but his tiring limbs reacted a hair more slowly every time.

Reginald's energy was boundless. His fists came down in a rain of fury.

Smoke covered his face.

Reginald went for the stomach.

Smoke guarded his belly.

Reginald smote his face.

The tremendous blows rattled Smoke's grey matter. In a break between blows, he said in a gasp, "Wow, I really am a great fighter."

"No, I am," Reginald replied. He had Smoke pinned. His body grew. His visage was Smoke's but more bestial. The seams in the fine clothing burst. Reginald became a Mr. Hyde version of Smoke and said from slavering jaws, "I'm going to break you into pieces, brother!" He started hammering Smoke into submission.

With his strength quickly fading, Smoke blocked with everything he had left.

Brother?

CHAPTER 41

AGONY. PAIN. THE ONLY THING holding Smoke together was the sweetheart suit. He blocked what he could but couldn't attack anymore.

Reginald had him pinned down by the neck. His powerful hands squeezed until Smoke's eyes bulged. "You are a difficult man to control, mortal. And frankly, I'm tired of holding back."

"I can see you're all puffed up about it." Through Reginald's steely vise-like grip, Smoke struggled to say, "It seems to me I got under your skin."

"You know, not so long ago, Kane and I had an interesting discussion. How do you control a mortal who does not fear death?" Reginald's eyes lit up. "You see, it's fear that holds your kind back. Not so long ago, more of you were quite fearless. Then the ones like you show up. Like a briar in the skin between our toes. Every step we take, the nagging is there. It's aggravating. Especially when it's so hard to remove. Like you, brother."

The rail vibrated beneath Smoke's neck.

Reginald turned his head. "I think a train is coming. Isn't that quaint?"

Straining, Smoke tried to speak.

Turning his ear, Reginald leaned down, relaxed his grip. "Go ahead. Say what you have to say, smartass."

Puffing for breath, Smoke said through his busted-up face, "It makes me think of one of my favorite movies." He regurgitated a supervitamin, one of the ones with a special coating Mal had made for him so it wouldn't dissolve. He crunched down on the pill and swallowed it again, saying, "It's called *Dark Territory*."

"Never heard of it, brother."

"Quit calling me that."

"The truth hurts, doesn't it, John." Reginald watched the distant train clatter down the tracks. "Hmmm, that's a slow one. But we might just have to take it."

The supervitamin kicked in. The blood in Smoke's veins caught fire. His heart pumped like a steam engine's wheels turning. Against Reginald's great strength, his neck popped up. He said, "Let me tell you about *Dark Territory* first. It's about this Navy SEAL named Ryback. A SEAL like I used to be." He took Reginald's wrists and shoved them away.

Reginald's lips curled back. Astonished, he said, "How are you doing that?"

In one fluid move, Smoke bent Reginald's wrists backward. It sent the shifter back on his heels. Smoke found himself free of the monstrous man. He sprang to his feet. "You see, Ryback is a master of aikido, a real bone breaker."

"I'm well aware of what aikido is." Reginald sneered. "It won't do you any good against the likes of me."

"Let's find out."

Fluid as water spiraling down, Smoke attacked.

Reginald tore into him. The bigger, stronger version of Smoke let loose with savagery.

Smoke moved with the prowess of a jungle cat. A flurry of punches and slaps peppered Reginald's eyes.

The shifter now seemed determined to tear Smoke apart. He grabbed Smoke and body slammed him on the ground.

But Smoke popped up to his feet, locked up Reginald's arm, and cracked it back. The elbow snapped.

Reginald howled.

Smoke shattered the doppelganger's knee with a stiff, powerful kick.

Reginald dropped.

Smoke put the shifter in a headlock.

Tearing at Smoke's arms, the doppelganger said, "My bones mend quicker than you can breathe. Your little pill will wear off. How long does it last, a minute? Hahaha—*urk*!"

With the muscles in his arms bulging against Reginald's supernatural might, fueled by the vitamin, Smoke cranked back. "You're going to die, Reginald!"

Reginald twisted his hulking frame like a bucking bull.

Smoke held him fast and squeezed with all his vitamin-induced strength.

The layers of packed muscle in Reginald's neck

slackened. His fingers clawed. He swam as if he was trying to surface for air.

Pouring it on with everything he had left inside him, Smoke let out a scream, "Yaaaaaargh!"

Reginald's spine gave. *Snap!* The body went slack.

Smoke let go.

Reginald lay on his back, staring up at the sky. His form reverted to that of the man Smoke had learned to hate so long ago.

The train clattered down the tracks, racing at about thirty miles an hour. Its headlamp glowed through the trees. Smoke picked up Reginald's body and approached the tracks. He looked down at Reginald. "So you heal up pretty fast, do you? I can't let that happen. Let me tell you about a new reality show I'm going to pitch." He tilted Reginald up so he could see the train. "It's called *Shifter Versus Train*. And you get to star in it."

Reginald's eyes turned into moons.

One second before the train passed, Smoke heaved Reginald in front of it.

The powerful locomotive splattered the body all over the tracks.

Smoke watched the big coal train chug by until the caboose was long out of sight. There was little to be found of Reginald. Not even his head. Feeling his energy start to drain, Smoke trudged up the hill. The climb became harder with every step. He found the SUV, gave it a look, and kept going. He needed to get back to Sid. It took more mind than muscle to make it up the hill. When he made it to the top, a luxury sedan waited with the engine running. Kane and Allison were leaning against it.

Kane applauded. "I'll be. You really are the one." Dressed in a maroon leisure suit, he walked right toward Smoke, who raised his swollen fists.

"You might want to take a look at the last guy who messed with me."

Kane hit him so hard the black sky turned red.

EPILOGUE

S ID HELD HER POUNDING HEAD. Propped up against
the metal wall of the shipping container with
people scurrying and moaning in the darkness, she
said, "Everyone, be still. We'll be okay." Ears ringing, she
pushed herself up. The bombs had rocked the building
and knocked her out. She wasn't sure for how long. All
she knew was it was hot and stuffy, like the armpit of
some hellhole.

I've got to get out of here.

She noted a slim crack of light through a seam in
the metal. She stepped on and over some people, saying,
"Excuse me."

"Sid?" said a pesky woman's voice.

She knew it immediately. "Asia?"

"Yes. What have you gotten me into now? Why do
I feel so sick? Ugh! I feel like I'm surrounded by giant
fish."

"You're in a shipping container," Sid said.

"Damn, I knew it. That's how I got over here in the

first place." Asia sighed. "What the hell am I doing in a giant sardine can?"

"It's a long story. At least your mouth made a full recovery." Sid found the handle of the container door. She shoved the lever up. It was stuck.

"What are you doing?"

Sid jumped. Asia had crept right up on her heels. "Geez, you're sneaky. I'm trying to open this door."

"Let me help." Asia's hands found Sid's and started toggling the handle. The mechanism gave. They pulled the lever.

Sid put her shoulder into the door. It cracked open a foot. Cool air kissed her sweat-drenched face. The light she'd seen came from a lone skylight that still gleamed among the rubble. Piles of building lurked up all around. Sid squeezed through, with Asia on her tail.

Asia's jaw hung. "Was there an earthquake or something?"

"It's a long story."

"Who are all those slimy people in there?" Asia took note of herself. "Uck, what happened?" She slung her arms. "It looks like Godzilla sneezed on me."

"We need to find a way out." Basing her direction on the doors of the container, Sid scanned the parking garage the way she remembered it. Lucky for them, part of the interior support hadn't completely given way, but she couldn't see any part of the stairwell or elevator. The ramp leading out of the garage had collapsed. Half the first floor lay inside the garage, covering the shipping container. It gave Sid a chill. If not for the container, they'd all have been crushed.

She climbed over the debris. A light flashed in the corner of her eye. She turned. A light beam glowed where the garage doors closed. She waved her arms and yelled, "Hey! Help!"

Asia mimicked her calls.

"Hey! Help!"

Sid made her way over the scrap-heap structure. Debris sprinkled down into the garage where the ramp dropped off from the outside entrance. Someone was on the other side scooting the rubble aside. When the chunk of cement cleared, a man poked his head inside. He shined a light in her face.

"Sid?"

"Cyrus?"

"Holy crap! I should have known I'd find you here. Are there any other survivors?"

"A bunch. Including Ted—and Rebecca."

Cyrus sat beside Rebecca, who was shivering in a blanket. Mal was with Asia, and the pair of them were doing the same. Ted hunched under his blanket next to Sid, not saying much. The FBI had spent hours getting the survivors out of the ruined building. All the walls and windows had been blasted out, but the structure still stood, a skeleton frame of its former self.

Cyrus kissed Rebecca's head. "I'm so glad you're alive. The other you died. I thought you and the baby were gone forever."

With a quizzical look, Rebecca said, "Baby?"

Sid's hand went to her abdomen.

Mal eyed her. "How are you feeling?"

"I'm just worried about Smoke. Can we talk for a moment?"

Mal looked at Asia.

"Go ahead. I'm fine now," the little woman said. "Just hungry. Don't these ambulances have any food? I want some fish sticks. And beer. Hey, big boy, you got any beer? You look like a drinker," she said to an agent.

After moving to a more private area, Sid caught Mal up with everything Reginald had told her about being pregnant. "And the baby? Can we run a test and find out?"

"Of course we can," he said with a reassuring look. "It won't take long to run it through a lab."

Her fingers dug into her palms. Life had been turned inside out again. She was faced with more questions than answers. And Smoke was gone. Her heart ached. "We have to find him."

"He's resourceful. I'm sure we will." He took her by the shoulders and squeezed them. "I can't thank you enough for saving Asia. For saving all of them. It's like a miracle, Sid. A victory. I swear, you can also count on me. With the clones gone, we've mortally wounded them."

"I know, but it feels hollow to me. They took Smoke. Vormus and Manson are gone. I want to know when the bodies are found. And what about A.V., Toad Man, and Night Bird? Do we still have eyes on them?"

"They were all secure last I checked a few hours ago."

"Good. We just need to figure out what to do with them."

An FBI sedan sped through the front gate. The tires ground to a stop on the shattered rubble and glass. The driver, Agent Jonnie Wok, exited with Smoke's rucksack in one hand and the Arabian sword in the other.

Sid rushed him.

Agent Wok made his way over to Cyrus. His eyes widened on Sid.

"Where did you get that?" she said.

"A few miles up the road. An SUV crashed over the hill."

"Did you see any other sign of Smoke?"

"No, but something got splattered all over the tracks. It looked like a man got hit by a train. Agents are still picking up the remains."

Sid's heart sank.

Jonnie Wok held out a sheet of paper folded up like a note. "I found this."

Sid's name was written on the note. She took it and opened it. The note read:

"Dear Sister, we have Smoke. Changes are coming. Once you're gone, he will be mine... Forever. Allison."

The dark adventure resumes in SMOKE HAPPENS, Book #9. Release date to be January 27th, 2017! Stay in touch at craig@thedarkslayer.com, www.craighalloran.com, Facebook, and Twitter.

ABOUT THE AUTHOR

Craig Halloran resides with his family outside his hometown Charleston, West Virginia. When he isn't entertaining mankind, he is seeking adventure, working out, or watching sports. To learn more about him, go to: www.thedarkslayer.com.

WORKS BY THE AUTHOR

Clash of Heroes: Nath Dragon meets The Darkslayer

The Darkslayer Series 1
Wrath of the Royals (Book 1)
Blades in the Night (Book 2)
Underling Revenge (Book 3)
Danger and the Druid (Book 4)
Outrage in the outlands (Book 5)
Chaos at the Castle (Book 6)

The Darkslayer Series 2
Bish and Bone (Book 1)
Black Blood (Book 2)
Red Death (Book 3)
Lethal Liaisons (Book 4)
Torment and Terror (Book 5)

The Chronicles of Dragon Series 1
The Hero, the Sword and the Dragons (Book 1)
Dragon Bones and Tombstones (Book 2)
Terror at the Temple (Book 3)
Clutch of the Cleric (Book 4)
Hunt for the Hero (Book 5)

Siege at the Settlements (Book 6)
Strife in the Sky (Book 7)
Fight and the Fury (Book 8)
War in the Winds (Book 9)
Finale (Book 10)

The Chronicles of Dragon, Series 2, Tail of the Dragon
Tail of the Dragon
Claws of the Dragon
Sword of the Dragon
Eye of the Dragon
Trail of the Dragon
Scales of the Dragon

The Supernatural Bounty Hunter Files
Smoke Rising
I Smell Smoke
Where there's Smoke
Smoke on the Water
Smoke and Mirrors
Holy Smoke
Up in Smoke
Smoke 'em
Smoke Out
Smoke Happens

Zombie Impact Series
Zombie Day Care: Book 1
Zombie Rehab: Book 2
Zombie Warfare: Book 3

CONNECT WITH HIM AT

Facebook: The Darkslayer Report by Craig
Twitter: Craig Halloran